BLACK MYTHOL

THE MISGUIDED

Copyright 2022

The Misguided: Black Mythology (Short Stories)
First Edition *
By: B. Hakeem Paul Morado

Printing : G&H Soho
ISBN 978-0-9990926-1-3 (Self-published)

This is a work is the blending between non-fiction with fiction. Names, characters, places, and incidents either are the product of the author's imagination or are used fictitiously. Any resemblance to actual persons, living or dead, events, or locales is entirely coincidental.

THE IDEA

The idea of Black Americans having an identity separate from their white or other ethnic counterparts has been a challenge for quite some time. The blending and mixing of diet, entertainment, and expression are the main ingredients that are a challenge to dissect. Such extractions requires a dissection of even the connection between our own Pre-American ancestors, Africans.

The Black American brought forth an enormous amount of intangible trades, habits and aspects of culture. We as a collective, share a nature of high volume of consumption and consumerism, yet still do not own large fabric manufacturing facilities, distilleries or health care agencies, which are major industries we partake. The remedy, I believe started back at the point where the first groups of African natives began to comprehend that they were more likely to never return home. It was at that time and forward on, the predecessors of Blacks would have needed extremes amount of therapy. Therapy to heal from the traumatic experience of being kidnapped, raped and physically and mentally abused. These critical times of healing would have been pivotal, making it less difficult for the modern Black male or female to adjust and adapt to the currents of American structures seen today.

As we moved into the world of television and media, Blacks were able to see a way of channeling this trauma into a form of expression. Self-expression became the rising trend of the Revolutionary Era for Blacks. From hair styles, wardrobes, and culinary talents, Blacks developed a unique language and communication between one Black American to another Black American. The Media Era spearheaded the visual glimpses of Black music and culture creating innovative ways to wear gold or clothing became a lifestyle. This injection administered by Black people shaped a world for the new way of attitude and approach. For some, it even created a armor of confidence. As the Black American trots into the Technology Era, we were encouraged, sort-of-speak, to keep up

with the rest of the world. Smartphones and futuristic gadgets gave us a sense of living in the same time and space as our counterparts. I believe what happen is the pressure from this change and agenda of White America, forced us to skip necessary steps as a collective in our healing.

In the world of Social Media, the world caught a good look into the homes and lifestyles of Blacks. And like many impressionable and misguided groups, a large group of us felt compelled to show a life of illusion. Stocking up on Nikes and Versace apparel along with outsourcing hair and skin products to feel accepted. By this time, if Blacks were given back the same years that were taken, the urge for such implosions would be minimal. There would be acres more of neighborhoods such as St. Albans, Baldwin Hills or Olympia Fields. I aim for the goal of Black neighborhoods to be truly reliant on themselves. Having primary ownership of their own, crops, water, cattle, clothing and shelter, would allow us to be truly independent. I believe this idea was brought on more intensely for me in the realm of dating outside my race. Majority of the casual or exclusive dates that were of White or other ethnicities, held a sense of stability, primarily financially. I noticed when I hit a financial and emotional drawback or mishap, that particular relationship began to diminish.

The safety net for many of our American counterparts, appears tightly seamed. Meanwhile, the safety nets for us relies on us helping complete strangers and distant relatives in a time of need. What one white adult parent can do for their child, would take an entire family within the Black household. I thought only my imagination can save me from moments of despair and inevitable failure. I feel that to create a structure of our lives progressing through hardship, we would need to start with our own belief system. A system of deities and spiritual beings exclusively connected to that of Black Americans. The concept gave me another

thought; intertwine the existence of these Black Gods to spirits, lateral or parallel, to that of other ethnic or cultural Gods within mythology.

In doing so, this will create a belief system so ingrained, that Blacks will no longer associate Gods like Aphrodite or Zeus as a primary thought for polytheistic deities. Gods spawned from the exclusive journey of body language, music and agriculture will have Blacks reassessing their belief system along with intentions of pursuing a passion or occupation. "Have they been here this whole time?" "How come I've never heard of these Gods!?" Questions I want the Black American to ponder as they become familiar with the existence of their own identity as well as their Gods.

Beginning

The Nero Gods: the Gods of Black culture and of Black shades. Living in the new American territory. Though a young mythology, the first of the Nero was Evelyn. She is a Goddess belonged to the lineage of Akongo, a Supreme God of the Congo located in Central Africa. She represents the Spirit of birth, resilience, and purity.

It is Evelyn's (known as Eve), bloodline that almost every Nero native in America arrives from. Eve made it a standard for Gods to stay in close connection with their believers and offspring. The oldest of Nero Gods are Dryden, Orizah, Piruphius and Lufkin. Dryden is a deity formed in the conflict of both African natives and American natives who share the same shade and culture, yet clashed during moments of communication. He is a spirit that bridges the gap between Nero generations in which their language is not native to that of the American dialects.

Piruphius, the God of Assembly and Unity. He was a soldier and leader of the Black Brigade. He led his soldiers through a fight between British and natives. His soldiers or Tribesmen, grew loyal and dedicated to the belief of aligning with those who resemble that of Piruphius. An alpha God who protects and provides. Piruphius often stayed celibate until his long romance with the Goddess Aria during the beginning of the 19th century.

In regard to the God of Foresight, Lufkin, gained notoriety during the 20th century. Though still the visual age of a teenager, Lufkin is a God that brought many Nero natives through troubled or misguided times. He can grant the capability for a mortal to see relatives in their dreams. Even strangers they may encounter years later. It is Lufkin, who gives the ability to mortals to travel a Godspeed within their translucence state. However, with all of his enchantments and powers, he can still fall for childlike tendencies, such as gullibility and lack of experience.

With these Gods essential to Nero mortals, they cannot operate without Orizah, the Goddess, of Nourishment and Substance. Though she is a culinary deity, she is also key for healing Gods and mortals with the blessing of spiritual nourishment such as meditation, comprehension and accountability. She is also known for being one of the first Goddess to integrate Neros and Elbrus Gods. As for the Nero Gods counterparts, they have lived for millenniums compared the Nero Gods whom lived centuries.

Known as the Elbrus Gods, these Gods were birthed in the Spirit of Supremacy; control and impulsive freedom. Drogheda, Potis and Cephalos were the oldest out of four siblings in the American land. Cephalos was the God of Psyche and Hold. He mastered the ability to form the structure of slavery in America with the help of the French and Dutch rulers support to capture Nero or African mortals. His sons, were the true forefathers of the Americas, George Washington, Lincoln, and Benjamin were his favored. The "Dead Presidents," became the most prominent, worshiped Gods, as currency shifts into the new century.

Potis, the God of Supremacy and Entitlement. His believers represent movements in the new land that reflect strong separation between his race and the Nero or Native. Potis believed if he can control women sexually, it can allow minimal distractions from female immortals or mortals. Drogheda, though a sibling, is also a lover to Potis. She is the Goddess of Lust and Hunger. She is held captive as a sexual slave to Potis in his fear of her becoming a ruler greater than him.

Drogheda would later birth offspring, Aunjanue, Spirit of Seduction and Temptation. The stories themselves are written within the nature of a Gods or Goddess journey. The timeline is meant to articulate the intersectional relationships between Gods and the in-

fluence of Gods; able to move forward, while going backwards. Mostly, Nero Gods were active throughout the time Africa natives arrived to the new lands. However, it isn't until the early 1900s, Nero Gods realize more than ever, mortals are key to their own existence. The stories themselves reveal Gods like Medusa, are only the most influential God to Nero mortals, after their Nero God shows favor to her. Essentially, Gods in this era are worshiped through the extension of clothing. Along with the distraction of the Elbrus or Greek God's, many Nero also face a God of bias and judgment, Drahmen. The God of Adaption, Adjustment, and Calculating. He lives in the space between *opportunity* and *obstacle*. The rules for Drahmen are clear to some Gods, but fall lost on mortals. Weaponed with a brass handle whisk with leather weaved together containing a steel ball, Drahmen makes sure to make his judgment felt. No mortal shall pass without the chaperon of another mortal or God of Elbrus pigment. Though Drahmen doesn't often state, Nero mortals have a higher chance of being successful if they're accompanied by a large group of their people and/or with a Nero God. Gaining access through his realm grants a God or mortal a blessing to what they aimed to achieve. He is not necessarily a key visual deity, but he is pivotal in a Nero's path.

Gods within the new land, birth offspring and adolescents through various forms. To dig deeper, this means Gods like Aria, the Goddess of Music and Nurture and Piruphius, God of Unity, creating a spiritual connection and romance between music and unity. Dryden, the God of language, births a son, Taurean. Taurean is birthed from bloodline of Language and therefore, he is the God of (*new*) language. A pivotal God in the history of America. He is truth to the rise and confidence of the Nero people in current generations. He was the first Nero God to get mortal tattoos and jewelry embracing his culture. Taurean being the leader of new language, he was spoken of by

his elders as, loud mouth, reckless and a silly adolescent. Though these thoughts may be true or not, Taurean remains the bridge for a crucial connection between Nero mortal men and women and him and his father.

Athena sent a servant to me. A servant that praised her deeply. A Demi-God, there was nothing unique about him. He was young, and weak-willed, so he relied on the voice of a vengeful being to learn my weakness and use it as his strength. She proposed he shall find me at rest during the day when the Sun was reaching its highest point.

Athena had the same goal as most Gods then; pursue to conquer territories and have praise over men and woman. It was such a bore to me, mortals believing one God's opinion over another without so much a thought to hear a other's side. Unfavored, I died that night. My head detached, but my soul lived. Traveling back through worlds, Perseus, used my head to kill off anyone who opposed him. He used the blood of my head to also heal himself. During his journey back to Athena, he unknowingly dropped the blood of Gorgon and the snakes that were birthed from my scalp. The one that lived all these years was *I,* and it was I, who made my way to the city of Algiers.

His name was Lord Hussein Dey, a Ruler of a small city in Algiers. He kept me around for a while to fend off mice, critters and men from his treasures. It wasn't until his exile I was able to make it to Naples. Most of the town at the time was rich with wheat, a primary diet of mines. I used to stay in an alley where a cook would leave dough and cheese for vagrants. Eventually, I grew and became hard to go unnoticed. I started to scare women and kids and families. I hated my self for this. Taking up space in a place I was unwanted.

That same chef would sometime have a driver take tons of wheat and dough in a wagon. It was this way, I found my means of transportation. One day when it was the darkest sky, I slithered into a crate. I noticed the driver became use to his routine, never quite inspecting the crates. I can hear the chef telling him to make sure he takes them to each drop off. The ride felt long, I had no idea where I was going. At one point, Matteo stopped for a break, I heard him talking to himself and then laughing. My guess is long drives required his mind to entertain his own company.

Matteo would make small stops and exchange bread for money. Sometimes more of a profit on the side. My weight may have been the deciding factor but what I heard next was concerning. Underneath me, was a scratching and wading noise. As the noise increased, the wheels underneath the wagon collapsed. He tries to pull over on a narrow road in a town. I had to think quickly, as I can hear him approaching the rear of the wagon. I jumped off the crate and rush under a rocky bush with cacti.

I heard him curse, fiercely and throwing rocks to provoke me. When I made it out the wagon the land seemed as if life was beginning to blossom. But after the warm season past, I saw very little activity and even heard less voices ring throughout these valleys. The town Naples was believed to be cursed by Perseus. Leaving hundredths of thousands of mortals dead from his massive earthquake as punishment of trades and praise to other Gods of Norse culture. It wasn't the only punishment they faced. A war was heard of some miles away and it was moving to this small town.

I spent a lot of time hiding and taking advantage of vacant homes. Many of the men that once lived there unfortunately did not return. Bombings and chaos became frequent. So much lost, I would hear their prays to their God as their death approached. As days pass, I became increasingly famished. I started eating abandoned bergamots and plants, but it wasn't enough.

I saw an elderly woman with small chickens which seemed like a good idea, but I figured if her only livestock goes missing, I shall find myself yet again to blame. I watched a man walk out his yard into a field. There was a small well he would get water from. I watched this for days before I felt it was safe enough to try and get a drink. On the day I finally decided, I heard a noise close by, so I ran into this small shed. I stayed there for another day or two, as my hunger caused confusion. Small tools and fabrics and hides sat dormant as I used them for shelter and warm. Later that day, I was able to get water and that's when I saw him. I scared

the older man who went to the well often. He dropped his bucket and keys out of his hand shouting, "Dios mio!" Staring at this massive snake. I sat still, beginning to shake in trauma. "Antonio!" His name I gathered from a mortal woman who frequently shouted to him from time to time.

I heard a noise one particular night sleeping, it was Antonio creeping into the shack I stayed in. I saw a hand and a light, and without second thought, I attacked him! I was destroyed, I never thought I would hurt Antonio, he was such a kind man who never brought me any harm. He provided me shelter as I scared off the hounds that roamed the night near his livestock. I never wanted to hurt him. I didn't see him, I saw Perseus, the pitiful man-child, trying to prove something. Maybe he's a descendant- or akin perhaps of Perseus! A thought to make my-self feel better of my actions in an anxious state. He yells, cursing me while tearing fabric from his shirt as he mends his bleeding hand.

I didn't see him for some time after that, not even in the home he lived in where the woman who shouted to him took care of their children. I felt a sense of responsibility to repair my broken trust. I stayed in prox-imity of his home to protect his family until he returned. The mother would come to the well with her young. She was careful and very para-noid. She spoke the language of the natives there. I found it hard to dis-entangle her complaints from statements through her day to day. Con-stantly calling her young ones names excessively. A name I heard over and over, "Gianni! Gianni!" She always cautioned him. He was an average size boy. In those moments, scolding fell on Gianni when blame needed to be given. However, I often grew jealous of the attention Gianni received.

During the winter, I spent most of my days sleeping, so I missed a lot of their daytime. A ball fell into the shed, knocking a wood panel on top of

me. Abruptly, I woke and heard children cackling. I heard a girl speak to her kin to grab the ball. That is when I saw him up close, creeping into the shed, he wasn't afraid, just uncertain. A young boy with full dark hair with a serendipitous spirit. He stepped closer but didn't notice me.

He reached over to grab the ball but jumped back from being startled from his father's tools falling, I moved further into the shed. He now noticed me, I think, I heard him say something and stood silently for a moment, awaiting a response and *sureness* of my presence. Gianni grew inquisitive, splitting his time from his siblings and the shed. He would come in seeking me, sitting next to me and telling me about his day. I could not understand him. His dialect was broken, but it was still pleasant to see his interest in me. "What is your name snake...? Where did you come from snake!? I shall call you Monica, I like Monica," Gianni expressed eagerly. Fascinated, Gianni leaned in closer, "You hava nice eye color Monica, a beautiful hazel." Staring at her eyes, he says, "God, your eyes! Your gaze at me." I allowed him to get comfortable with caressing my skin. I rubbed against his legs to initiate a gesture of trust, something I've never done with Antonio.

He felt compelled to pick me up, I couldn't help but feel uneasy at this. I struggled and wiggled a lot just to get out of one palm only to land onto the next. Before leaving he comes back, "Monica, I have something for you". It was a fabric as a gift. He cleaned an area and laid me on it to keep warm. My body started to feel different during this time, as if I had hands to hold or toes to wiggle. I felt I could breathe again, as a human. With a set of lungs, I started shedding skin rapidly and began growing hair. A mortal feeling again, this was my second time taking my first steps. It was hard at first, but I could see legs and they were challenging to walk on. I looked down to notice blood flowing from between my two legs. I used the cloth Gianni gave me. I was now a young girl again.

Weeks later, Gianni in tears, runs outside with his brother. Gianni pulls him in the direction of the abandon shed. Santo shouts in Italian, "Dove stai andando!?" Gianni mopes towards the shed only to see a small girl standing in the distance. He paused briefly, wiping his eyes to take a second glance- "She's gone!" He replied. His brother Santo confused, as he pulls Gianni back into the house. Gianni runs into his room, crying, his family mourning their sibling, Tiffany. She was their youngest sister that Gianni was closest to, being the youngest boy. One night Gianni sneaks out again to try and find Monica, he whispers loudly as animals howl in the distance. "Monica!" He continued, "Where are you!?" Walking out of the shed only to be frighten by his mother. Gianni tries to explain to his mother who is Monica, but it's no use. In rage and concern, she shouts that it's a *"friend "* he created in his mind in-light of his sister passing.

Gianni followed up with many attempts to see if Monica was still in the shed only to bring more attention to his mother by waking her with noise in the night. His mother, in frustration, brings her children along to light a match onto the shed. Gianni cries intensely, screaming at his mother as his sister and brother try to contain him. In a fragile yell, he calls for her, "Monica!? Please! Monica! I'm so sorry!" After his personal lost of his sister and now the thought of Monica being killed, Gianni fell into more of a depression and became disconnected from his mother. After long stint in his room, his mother started to raise worry. Coming into his room he shared with Tiffany, to see if Gianni wanted some biscuits to console him. As days progress, he began working close with his mother, helping her with her clothing business, staying busy with minor duties with organizing patterns and fabrics. He started to show exceptional growth and skill as a junior seamstress in his mother's shop, landing freelance gigs. Years passed, Gianni never mentioned Monica aloud, but called to her in his heart daily.

While preparing to move, Gianni goes with his mother into town to shop for fabric and books. His mother goes off with his siblings into the shops while he trots from shop to shop browsing. Walking past an alley, he sees a girl no older than fourteen or fifth-teen years of age. "Ehi, stai bene!?" A bit louder and stern, "Ehi ragazza, stai bene!?" As he walks forward, closer, he notices she's barefoot wrapped with a large fabric around her. As he is about to run for help, the girl mumbles a word. With a long pause, Gianni turns back and replies, "Wait, what? What did you just say!? How do you know my name!?" Standing shocked, he looks and not a moment too soon he speaks aloud, your eyes, they're beautiful- suddenly, with a glow in his heart and tears in his eyes, Gianni questions in a slight whisper, "Monica!?"

His mother calls for him before he can retrieve an answer. While turning back to see the girl, she's disappeared. "What were you doing!?" Gianni's mother demands. "Ah, ano-nothing," Gianni still perplexed about what he thought couldn't possibly be true. On the way home, he tries to explain to his siblings about a girl he seen. They laugh as Santo, his brother, suggest to their mother, "It's time for Gianni to get out more!" His mother looks at Gianni with a long stare of certainty and replies, "You need only focus on school Gianni!" During his daily routine at the shop, Gianni felt a burning desire to find out more about this mysterious woman. Old enough, he started suggesting to his mother he can do the weekend runs to the shops all by himself.

At first, there was no success, Gianni tried looking in every alley or street or back block for this woman. Through desperation and wariness, he stumbled into a local library for rest and information. "Excuse me Miss, I've been looking for a woman, she has dark hair and the most beautiful hazel eyes". The receptionist, unfazed and over the day entirely, slides across the front desk a book of Italian nude woman portraits. Gianni rushing, "No, forgive me, Miss! A woman outside, she wears a

large blanket she's barefoot… maybe you seen her?" As he waits for her reply, a man walking pass, overhears the conversation. "Hey! You boy, I seen her," walking to Gianni to speak over his shoulder quietly, "You're talking about the girl who stares at you like she can kill you with just a look in her eyes!" In desperation, Gianni replies, "Yeah, yes!" The older man takes him outside to point to a street. Driving in that direction, he spots her! Gianni hopped into his mother's Fiat, speeding down the road. Smashing on the brakes, Gianni slides into a curve, rushing out to see her.

Gianni at a loss for words, is shocked, as he sees Monica standing on the side of a fruit shop eating a rotten apple. Getting Monica's attention, he smiles, "Alright, don't move!" Gianni rushes back to the car and brings Monica a piece of clothing to wear to change into back at the library. Coming out of the restroom, the dress slightly abstract on Monica, Gianni says, "Great! Now put these on, they were my sisters' shoes, I think they will fit you perfectly." I mothered a thousand thoughts. I couldn't say what I was thinking. Watching Gianni's face, I knew it was the spirit of a man who wanted me to be safe, not the look of many men with lust. After all this time, he found me, this young derelict girl feasting off rubbish from the leftovers of café shops and food stands. I couldn't find my way back to him after his mother burnt the shed. I managed to force my legs to move one in front of the other that night. Standing outside the restroom door, this was all that was running through my mind, I didn't speak, I just looked and smirked. Though I grew, I still haven't gathered the gift of words. Gianni sits Monica down in a chair as he pulls out a few grammar books to help Monica. He responds, "Alright, so first words to learn are vowels…". As he taught me the Italian alphabet, I noticed we were always in monastery-like buildings. I found it unique at first-romantic even, but grew bored, so I decided to take Gianni outside to show him my ways of absorbing information. Pointing at everything I could see, he laughs, "…a car, …barista, …a house." Mon-

ica, a quick learner, still had ways away from speaking fluently again.

At the beach, sitting in his car, he stared at me for a while, at first, I thought maybe he possessed a power. I often felt *seen* when he stared this way, I gather this is what he felt in return as a young boy. He pulls a paper out of his sketch book, handing it to Monica nervously, "I need you to tell me or better yet, show me, what you are." As I took the paper and pencil, I believed what he wanted was not a portrait, but for me to reveal myself. Something I found more difficult than I imagined.

A surprise to me, my artistic capabilities were better than my speech. Stuttering with a laugh, I replied, "This… mi." As he deciphered the drawing, he stood there holding it up the paper to the Sun. A sketch forming a snake, morphing into a lightly-shaded woman with shoulder length hair, and a charm-like-jewel tied on the end of a her locked hair. Her eyes, a glowing hazel and defined brow-ridge. He made it a routine, seeing Monica on his days off, often taking her to his favorite library to study. He sat up all night remembering the drawing Monica showed him. Restless, Gianni then dumps books from the library onto his desk. Intrigued, he sees a book of a photo of a woman with snakes immersed from her head on the cover with a word titled, "Gorgon". Opening the book, Gianni could retire until he finished reading it that night.

He was hooked; Medusa, the beautiful hazel-eyed Goddess who turned men into stone. Gianni couldn't believe it; pieces of Monica was sketched throughout history. Her face on flags, armor and sculptures. Gianni grew an idea in his mind. This eventually pulled Gianni into Greek mythology. Back together again over the weekend, Gianni, as a curious man ask, "So, your lover was Poseidon!? Gianni chuckles, "How was that?" Monica frustrated and triggered, "Agghh! Enough!" Gianni shook at

the earthly tone. He turns to her to see her distraught. "Siento, Monica." Trying to console her, she pulls away and continues walking, not saying a word, all the way to the courtyard. Gianni heading back into the shop spots his mother without a pause in her work, "Gianni, where's the dress for Gloria, I left it in the car, I do not see it". She can tell by the look on his face whatever he would say would be a lie. She puts down her chalk and pins. "I need you to understand! I am trying to protect you! I know you like this girl, but she's trouble, she's a distraction Gianni! Sneaking out to see her is getting in the way of your work and studies."

Days turns into months after Gianni begins to build garments from sketch to ready-to-wear. The book, Medusa, gave Gianni an inspiration into not only mythology but architecture and lifestyle. After returning home from Milan, he tells his family he's ready to start his own line. He brings his sister and brother in the room discussing this full proof plan. In this plan, his sister, Donna is shocked at how organized and passionate Gianni's become. Gianni expresses, "The culture Donna, it's our lifestyle, silks and drapes and sex!" Donna laughs, "I see Gianni, but what will momma think? It's very modern Gianni, very different than what momma creates in her shop." He interrupts with excitement, "Yes Donna! It is modern! The world needs a re-birth of these Gods; incorporating them into apparel, giving them life again. I need to make some new pieces, you'll see!" As his mother's shop is closing, he hides me around the corner as he sneaks inside from the back entrance. Fabric and the smell of cigarettes lingered. I was panicking, I felt I would see his mother again, she was the only one who noticed I was the *young girl.*

Sitting on a stool, he puts on his mother's radio, a foreign voice introduces a song that was soothing and mellow. He stands me up to measure me. First, my feet to spine, my spine to my neck, then, across my torso, and my arm. I was mesmerized by his passion. It was so

meditative to watch the scarlet silk sliced away like a hot blade to flesh. He threw large bodies of fabric over a female shaped frame. I assumed this was a mold of me, however, the breast area was unlike mines.

"It was not a marriage of proper form. We shared a concealed love, a forbidden love." Cutting more fabric, Gianni looks up, quite thrown off, he responds, "Que?" Monica explains again calmly, "You asked me about him, my Lover. He was a God, powerful amongst the Sea, he knew it was forbidden, but we could not resist the temptation, even as Gods. He was stubborn but a mighty Olympian. If he held a grudge, he sort you out vengefully." As Monica, explains, Gianni places the garment on her, stitching the dress by hand. Monica walks over to a large ornate floor mirror. The dress pressed against her skin as she turns to observe Gianni's techniques. Gianni was right about one thing the silk complimented my chic curves with a concealed slit along my calve. "So, what do you think? Do you like this?" Gianni folding his arms, one holding his head, while he slowly taps his foot against the sewing pedal. "Why…!" In tears, Monica takes a moment. "Why, yes, of course, it's beautiful…" "Well, it's for you Monica, I made this dress for you." Monica leaned forward, avoiding her tears from falling on the dress as she laughs with Gianni.

He quickly grabs a tissue. He stayed in the shop till the early hours when his mother would arrive. Anxious Gianni, waits for his mother and sister to walk in as they discuss his garments, "So what are you going to have on your tags…" Donna asks impatiently. Sitting, Gianni twiddles his fingers, moments after flicking his pencil between his lips and suddenly he turns around to grab a book. Sketching a concept, he then rips it off the sketch pad. Gianni mother asked, "Who or what is that Gianni!?" "Well, it's someone I wanted you guys to meet," Gianni nervously opening the door, "I want you guys to meet Monica, she is my muse." Gianni's moth-

er jumps up cursing him and throwing anything she can towards Monica "Why are you here! Now that my son is doing good, you want to interfere with his process and growth," Francesca says angrily to Monica. Gianni interrupts, "Mom!" "-Don't *Mom me* Gianni! She's a curse I swear, she will ruin you!" Gianni pleads to his mother, "Momma please, give me a chance, give her a chance, give this a chance, it will work!" His mother decided on chance out of love for Gianni. The garment Gianni made for Monica, was reproduced for selective clients through his mother's shop. This template dress started Gianni's brand. Undertaking their fathers surname, Giannis' brand, Versace, starts to thrive as flagships throughout the city of Milan to Florence to Rome are produced.

Gianni mother stays behind, giving him her blessing, she sees him off. Beginning his travel, Francesca looks over to Monica standing behind Gianni, then quickly, looks back at Gianni and smiles. They rejoice, they cry, as she tells him to take care of himself and be safe. During travel to America, Donna, Santo, and Gianni buys a house in the Southlands. It became the staple for the brand. Guest from friends, family and even celebrities; Nymphs, Legends and Icons, were able to spend days and even nights in their stunning 8-bedroom 10-bathroom mansion. This was the time of their lives, money and social success poured in as Gianni became more than a human but an Icon. In honor of her being his inspirational muse, Gianni surprises Monica with her own wing of the house. Gloomy drapes and pastel colored structures throughout the hallway. Eagerly rushing Monica through each room to show her the amenities. They reached a balcony that looks down to a small courtyard. Gianni speaks, "…and look, it's a pit full of snakes, don't you love it," seeking Monica's approval. Gianni can see Monica's excitement, "Alright fantastic, quick! I have someone downstairs whose dying to meet you!" As Monica sits for coffee, Madonna is brought into the courtyard to join

Monica. With a slight bow Madonna greets Monica, "It's a pleasure to finally meet you. I understand you're new here... welcome!" Monica replies, "...too America?" "No, your Suprema, I mean in this new body. You're ravishing, one of the most stunning Goddess' I've seen here, almost more than the Glamour Goddess herself! You've been gone for a long time Monica; your followers have been yearning for your return! I want to introduce you to someone, he's ready to bring you an enormous amount of believers; souls that will marvel at your mind, your body, and your spirit."

Madonna continues, "I heard about your arrival from the Goddess Drogheda. It's a golden era baby! There's enough out here for all of us. Followers here are prepared to die for you Monica, making you a God amongst Gods! Monica shocked of this construct, intrigued, "...in my time, I was written about; poems and sonnets, how can this new worship translate?" Madonna snickers, "Gods are worshiped through fashion in this new world. You're becoming the most valued and most worshiped Goddess everywhere, geesh, even more than Nike." Dipping her spoon, Monica looks up, "What do you want in return?" Madonna showing a smile, "I want to become *more*, Monica. A *Saint*, and you'll have the potential to direct religious power players and persuade them into that very belief. This parallel belief will guarantee you'll be stronger- much stronger and loved by Gianni more than you ever were before, as *I* live for eternity."

Monica sits on the thought for a moment, before she can speak- Madonna shouts, "I'm hosting an event this weekend, bring Gianni, he'll love it, it's good for the *brand*. It'll be good for him to meet a *diverse* group of faces. They have more money than God and believe me... they love women like you and me. Having their offspring is also one of the perks but some Gods oppose it. You'll find out soon, their skin is the source. I want to give you something. Madonna hands Monica a charm formed

into a ring made of jade. As Monica holds her hand out, "This ring was given to me from a High Priest. It is something he wanted me to give you. This ring contains your original blood as the Goddess, Medusa."

As Madonna exits, paparazzi and fans, stand outside awaiting to see Monica. As she leaves, she turns, "You see, your believers are growing already."

Monica decides to take Madonnas offer to the event. Upon walking in, Gianni, Monica and Madonna are introduced to several Gods and Goddess alike. Monica is stopped by Madonna, who introduces her to gentlemen by the name of Lesane. Madonna, explains, "Young Lordress, this is Lesane, the God I wanted you to meet," as she walks away taking her hand off Monica's shoulder. Lesane was a Demi-God of Spoken Truth and Expression. His father Henos often stayed close. Monica however, found Henos attractive, but was off-put by his presence. As Lesane pulls Monica to the side, Monica suggests she speaks with Lesane privately. Henos warned Lesane to be wary of his involvement with Monica. What Lesane wanted was for his voice to be heard globally. His offer was bringing her fellow theists, in return for favor and blessing. He speaks, "I hear you grant the gift of Eternity. I believe Madonna brought you up to speed!?" Monica brings him closer to whisper in his ear, while putting the small ring on her finger. A strong surge passed through her body. The ring was able to bring her spirit of Medusa back into her body. Medusa knew the language of the Nero, for she was also a child of Nero lineage. In seconds, Medusa is reborn. Medusa caress Lesane's hand and speaks, "One kiss and one bow, the favor is yours, in return I ask for million souls and your words will outlive your soul and your soul will outlive your body."

Lesane began to praise Medusa, and in doing so, his believers, followed suit. Medusa sees Gianni walking out with a man holding hands. In the heat

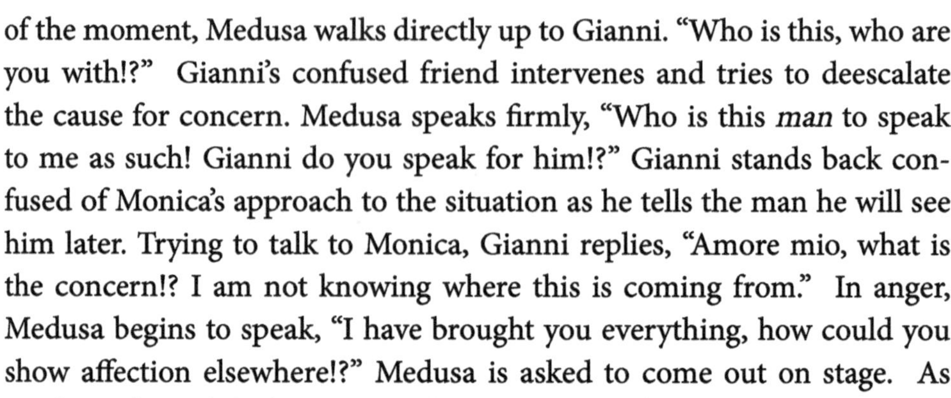

of the moment, Medusa walks directly up to Gianni. "Who is this, who are you with!?" Gianni's confused friend intervenes and tries to deescalate the cause for concern. Medusa speaks firmly, "Who is this *man* to speak to me as such! Gianni do you speak for him!?" Gianni stands back confused of Monica's approach to the situation as he tells the man he will see him later. Trying to talk to Monica, Gianni replies, "Amore mio, what is the concern!? I am not knowing where this is coming from." In anger, Medusa begins to speak, "I have brought you everything, how could you show affection elsewhere!?" Medusa is asked to come out on stage. As a token of good faith, Lesane takes a moment. "So, I want everyone to welcome this lady, this Queen, this Goddess… Medusa!" Lights flash all around the stadium, over hundreds of thousands of fans bow at her glory.

Medusa can feel her strength increasing. She gained the ability to convince men to perform acts and follow her every desire. Medusa slightly embarrassed, she couldn't quite grasp the rapid growth of her spells and enchantments. The men all froze in the crowd in *Ah*, of her beauty. Gianni overhears talk that Monica is Medusa. Heartbroken and unsure, Gianni tries to convince Medusa, "I ask you never use these elements against me my love. To be a puppet of love is a curse many wish to die from. I want to show you my love without such spells to woe me." Medusa feeling more of an immortal disconnect, she simply replies, "Never will I, my dear." As Medusa powers grow, so does the distance between her love. Medusa began to grow her own independence from Gianni. A man approaches Medusa during the event with a drink. "Good evening, your Suprema, my name is Andrew."

Medusa and Andrew began a rapport. Medusa noticed he's somewhat impressionable. His flaw was her advantage as Andrew became increasingly devoted to Medusa wishes in return for being rich and notable. Medusa concludes, "If this is done for me, I will make you more famous

than Gianni himself." Desperately, Andrew pleads, "Yes! My love, for you, Anything!" She follows Gianni and his partner into an adult nightclub, she enters unnoticed and unseen. Spying on Gianni, Medusa is enraged even more. Men in lust with men as the air was filled with Hermes spirit, a God who was fond of the same interest. Medusa could not control her emotion as she approached Gianni. In a rage, "Its forbidden to be a man and lover of men. Only Gods can, you are no God, Gianni!" "Okay, lets hold on for one minute-," Antonio, a partner of Gianni, sternly interrupts, right before being choked by Monica. With little to no effort she throws him into a wall. Gianni runs over to Antonio seeing cuts and scrapes from the mirror he was thrown into. Gianni burst into tears, "You need to leave! Just go!" Meeting with Andrew that night, Medusa gives word that this needs to be done immediately. Earlier that next morning, home, Gianni knocks on Medusa's door. With no answer he speaks into the lock, "I'll be back soon, I need to walk to the shops, when I get back, we can talk about everything!?"

Medusa hesitated to reach for the doorknob. She falls into deep thought. "My heart was too proud. I couldn't see the little boy I once witness care for me with such curiosity. He was different, he could never worship me the way I wanted. My awareness did not fail, I too, could not love this man anymore, he made me more than a lover; a Ruler, a Goddess in his eyes he could never truly connect with. He was right, I was no longer that snake that would slither, I am now strong wo"-

-A gunshot goes off! I went to the balcony, crows and doves flew as voices rose towards the front of the house. My hands squeezed the banister so hard; I could hear the wood internally crippling. "What have I done?" I began to question myself. I couldn't hear my own thoughts anymore, as sirens blared down the street, I could hear Donna screaming and banging on the door to warn me of what has happen. For a split second, I heard no door knocking

and no voice. Footsteps approached as I turned around slowly, I wondered what he was doing here. "Contrary to what you may think Medusa, there are rules in this new land. We have an agreement, no mortal dies from or by our hand. Medusa chuckles slightly, "It wasn't my hand Hermes!" Hermes draws his blade in response, "A mortal coaxed by a God cannot be punished for the sin committed. As she curse in her native tongue "iregimi-halehu! ānite ina yachī sēti wusha ātēna!" Medusa rushes in. Hermes using the reflection from his blade as a mirror, uses her gaze against her, turning her into stone instantly. Andrew Cunanan was able to receive favor from Medusa but upon committing suicide, was unable to obtain immortality.

Within the next few decades, change occurred, and the Versace mansion was transformed into historical grounds. Upon opening the door, the sales rep greets two gentlemen, "Good afternoon, may I help you with any-thing!?" Walking in with their heads down, they don't reply but just nod. Walking towards the back, the salesman calls for security to remain aware of the gentlemen that just entered. Standing impatient, one of the men re-ply, "We good boss, just let me get a size 10 in all three of these…" They stand with a long pause. "Yo bruh! We need size 10's! What the hell is yah problem!" Tensions climb as reps and manager approach the men. Man-ager approaches discreetly, "Sirs, we need you gentlemen to exit quietly please-" "Fuck no nigga! Size ten! All three! Thank you! As a matter fact throw a belt in there, too" as they sit down on the couch. The manager sig-nals to bring the shoes out. They open the boxes once, while one of the men walks up the counter the other puts a pair of to inspect the sneakers. "Can we get that belt we asked for, please!? Thank you?" A bit shaken, the clerk replies, "Thank you for shopping at Versace, enjoy the rest of your day."

Laughing uncontrollably, "Yo, you heard that scary bitch!?" "Yea like what the hell is that shit even about, calling security! 'Like bruh, if I wanted to

rob you, I would have." As both chuckle, they walk down the street to a loud protest, "We want justice! We want Peace!" Continuing, the men look at each other and decide to join the march. Walking aside of the march, they notice a guy a few feet in front of them, "Hey, hey bruh, say, where'd you get that shirt, that shit hard," he replies, "Oh good looking, this is vintage man, throwback Tupac." The young men observe, he is also wearing a similar belt and shoes. "Yea we see man, you even got the big Medusa on your belt and all that." The march grows louder as the crowd roars collectively, "Black lives matter! Black live matter!" The young men join in as their energy and intention increases. Five thousand Nero, chanting but wearing and worshiping *her*. This unknowingly, creating a calling to the Goddess herself. What Lesane did was leave behind an army of Nero men and women to seek a new leader. "I couldn't see anything, but I can hear loud and clearly, my name, my souls calling onto me, I had an opportunity."

Madonna, a Goddess, more expressive and much more of a vixen. She ruled over the *Teasers*, after making explicit music videos. She was crowned Queen of Pop. She was able to bring the Teasers into a world of commercial status, at least that was her perception. Drogheda was now of the older generation, but needed to stay relevant in the new world. In making Madonna a Demi-God under her, she would gain national praise, yet again. She reaches out to her, allowing Madonna to become a Goddess of Seduction and Tease. Drogheda admired her ability as a dancer and performer.

Madonna found inspiration by watching the Nero Teasers. The idea of sex in tandem with dance. She aroused herself as a performer more than the idea of a being with a man. She became close with the believers of the Goddess Aria. Madonna attended an erotic club one night. Walking through the crowd, she overhears a man in the corner with a woman. They begin to shout at each, "Yes! Yes! You love it!? I'm like a virgin baby!" This gave Madonna inspiration to create a song, "Like a Virgin." In the height of this song, Madonna caught a lot of attention from Nero men, mostly Gods. One God in particular was Henos.

The song brought his attention to Madonna. She began to fall in love with Henos. He was God of New Culture and Modern Nero Music. He mingled with several crowds and kept a demeanor that often was accepted in some areas oppose to others. Madonna dated Henos until she found him back with his lover, Afeni. Afeni was a mortal and was that of Icon status and favored by the Nero Gods. She was a pivotal figure in the movement for civil rights under Dryden's army. Seeing them both out walking, Madonna approaches Henos in anger, "How the hell could you!? You fucking asshole!" As he walks away, Afeni intercepts, "Hey, hey, Queen!" Trying to calm Madonna, "What do you think you're doing!?" Madonna replies, "I don't owe you anything or any explanation!" A laughable Afeni responds, "Oh yes, you sure do honey! You owe all of us Nero women

who raise and feed and nourish these young Nero boys and men. I've watched you: Seducers, Sloars and Teasers, just like yourself, come into my peoples land and infiltrate for your *God*! Your Aunjanues and Marilyns! Infiltrate with knowledge and resources!" Afeni continues, "Oh, oh, that's not you!? Oh really! Well do more as a Goddess than use your pussy to sway the minds of the impressionable Nero men. You say you care, you say you're an ally!? Show me, show yourself, actually do more for my people if your true intentions are beyond a shallow aspect of stealing these mens melanin! *Queen!*"

Madonna grew affected by Afeni claims. She made her way to see her mother Drogheda for answers. "I need to know, what's greater than what I am now!? Having the qualities of a siren or witch isn't doing enough, I need to be more!" Drogheda looks in shock, "My dear, I haven't been fully transparent, I act as your God-Mother, essentially, I gather your true mother will have more answers for you." Confused Madonna ask, "Well who is my mother!?" Drogheda looks over and walks to her study with Madonna, "Well your mother in terms of bloodline, over several centuries has been connected to the Suprema, Medusa."

Madonna anxiously excited, "Her grave... Where do I find it, is it in Pacentro!?" Drogheda pessimistically replies, "No, I know you've been told that, but her resting place is in the motherland of the Nero people." Madonna travels to go see the grave site. When she arrived, she was met with paparazzi and fans. Much of the world and Madonna for that matter had no idea of the connection between her and Medusa. Entering the Cathedral, she spots a Priesthood approaching her. With a slight bow, they greet Madonna, "It's an honor to meet you Queen and Goddess." Walking behind Madonna, the Priests speaks of Medusa reign of power and personal effects that have lasted for centuries. "We believe as a descendant, she would not worry of her belongings in your

possession!" It was a ring, a jade stoned ring with what appeared to be blood encased in the stones interior. It was said by the Priest, if the resurrected were to wear the ring, the spirit of Medusa can return and cast almost any spell or enchantment. Madonna takes the ring and approaches the tomb of the Goddess. While kneeling, she says a prayer and unexpectedly, speaks a language she herself never spoke before. She falls backwards as the Priest come to her aid. Madonna looking on in shock stands up and decides to stand outside. The High-Priest gathers his thoughts handing Madonna some water. "My Queen, there are many unanswered questions, it could be your spirit is connected, you possess the powers of Nero, we are not sure. But what we do know is now you possess the Gorgon Ring. With this ring, she will demand many sacrifices; of the world and of Gods alike. May you operate with caution, my Queen.

We see your influence here amongst the people. Your spirit here can help the community and the country in an instrumental way." Madonna looks around to see the natives and children shuffle through the town looking for food and shelter. In an instance, Madonna figures a plan to grow beyond her current status. When Madonna returns to the states she creates a song, "Like a Prayer." A strategy to rebrand herself as powerful and spiritual connected being. During her time back, many of the Elbrus Gods demanded a council meeting. Skadela, the Goddess of Facade, disliked her ways, after seeing her frolic with Nero Gods, seeing this as tasteless and raunchy. "I say, yea, you can like them sure! But never have children with them, they're animals! You might wind up a junkie or a sex-crazed slave to those monkeys. They will get you pregnant and neglect their young."

Drogheda intercedes, "What is clear is this, if not careful you can make a temporary choice become a permanent decision with that of the Nero. Many of us Gods who are not of Nero pigment won't socialize publicly with them. They have their own rules and practices and when things become bad for them, will you stand by their side, or ours? Madonna continues, "My decisions are based on character not color! Their personality, their aura, their spirit is what pulls me. You guys sound old. This is the new age. The age of blending!" An impatient Skadela, "No we are not old, we are wise, you are trying to play a saint, we only answer to one, the one Cephalos shares secrets with. Know and respect your history here in this land!"

As the interrogation concluded, Drogheda approaches a displeased Madonna. "My attempt was not to bash you, but to maintain an alliance. I hope your journey brought you answers to your questions." Madonna responds, "Yeah! I have my answers I know what I need to do. You sit there and play the political bout because you are still bound to Potis, I am bound to no one." Drogheda in disappointment, "Regardless of my ties and enslavement, you're a prisoner to your own ego. I pray your shackles are broken with minor injuries." Sarcastically, Madonna replies, "Likewise!" To add insult to injury, Madonna began dating Lesane. Lesane was a Demi-God and son to Afeni and Henos. Madonna gained word of the arrival of Gianni, he was the designer who used Medusa as a symbol for his clothing brand. Madonna reached out to him and was informed that the impossible was a reality. His lifelong muse, Monica, was rumored to be a resurrection of the supreme Medusa.

She invited Lesane to meet her ancestor and gave her the ring. What Lesane was blind to was he was the first sacrificial lamb to Medusa in the new land. Madonna knew Medusa needed a new group of followers in the new world. Madonna never told Medusa who she was to her, but allowed the elements to unfold for themselves playing off of the Gods habits and behaviors. Some years later, Madonna, returns to a memorial for Lesane. Many of his peers and Gods were in attendance. His father, a God, Piruphius, his grandmother Aria and Afeni. Afeni approaches Madonna, "Oh

my goodness! You have two beauties with you! I believe he would of been proud of his offspring!" A serious Madonna replies, "Ah no, these aren't his children." "Oh, ok, so another Nero fella I suppose!" Afeni assumes. Madonna tone raises, "No! Look! I have done what was needed, I have traveled to the motherland and adopted these two. I feel for a God to truly show their mark, they need to impact mortals in a major way!"

Afeni looks at Madonna, then down to her kids as they stand slightly behind Madonna's legs. She then laughs in a burst, "Ha haha! Oh my goodness girl! You took your ass to the motherland to buy some Ethiopian kids so you can feel better about yourself!? How did you even find them!? Out of the back of magazine? Ha ha, ok, let me find myself…" Walking away from Madonna, Afeni concludes, laughing, "Ha, I guess you-tha' Black Madonna now!"

After the Civil Rights War, many of Aunjanue's Hybrids, traveled with either Piruphius men to the west or settled in the east with Dryden's men. Offspring from the previous Hybrids were quite unique. These modern nymphs were called Teasers. They fed off the low self-esteem and compliments from men. They loved gold, pearls, fancy dinners and often booze. They were more equipped and knowledgeable in this era. These women had the ability to extract almost anything from a man. Aunjanue, free from Potis spell, decides to join the new Hybrids.

Most of the Teasers showed favor to her when she became an erotic dancer. Learning from the Nero women who performed, one would say, "You have to climb the pole with your soul, not just your hands." They gifted her with erotic toys, jewels and praised her with a ceremonial dance. It was the Neroian women that informed Aunjanue of the consequences of having several sexual partners. One dancer expressed, "Yea, you're a Goddess, so you can't catch anything we can, but you sure can definitely *feel*. Feeling of souls and energies and that can fuck with you". They believed those who carried a bad spirit can transmit energy through saliva, intercourse and even entering a persons home. The dancer continued, "Energy never dies, only transfers."

Aunjanue found therapy in the gifted toys. It was stimulating for her. It gave her a sense of arriving to a climax without the dealings of men and their hangups. She found herself dancing throughout multiple venues in the South and Eastlands. Aunjanue wore a lightweight baroque armor shield on her left breast, garments fancied into a lingerie and her hair color from variations of yellow, brown or pastels. While visiting her local venues, she sees a regular sitting in the corner. He was dismissive. With a drink on his table and blunt in his hand. She makes her way over to him. She whispers in his ear wrapping her hands around his waist, "Hey honey, I see you here often, what are you looking for!?" He responds blowing smoke, "For you, I suppose."

She found him attractive. "There was a sense of passion in him. The idea that he wanted me but didn't show it," Aunjanue thinks to herself. Going against her own rules, she offers him a sexual favor in the back room. Instead, he suggest leaving with Aunjanue. In her home laid potions and wine on her a table. Scented citrus candles from the south which was used to eliminate emotional stress. Her curtains were linen, along with her bed sheets. Bringing the man into her room, he made love to her. It was the first time she climaxed from a man. The emotional connection was there. She cuddled behind him for a moment before getting up. After putting on tea, Aunjanue ask, "So where are you from!?" He explains, "I came a long way. I use to be a part of a Tribe out west. I was abandon at a young age but now I stay *here* hurdling cattle for my father. Well, actually my step-pops." The conversation continues as Aunjanue finishes her tea. She grabs his hand and walks him to her bathroom as they both get the tub filled with peonies, oat and milk. She ask, "Do you know your biological parents!?" The man speaks, "I know many soldiers told me my father was a great warrior, he had a confidence to him; a swag. He was in charge of a great Tribe and led men to independence.

My moms, she was a pioneer, I heard. Free from what others thought and led a movement for woman to have a voice. That's all I know really." It then hits her, "at the club we don't really do names, but what is your name I must know!?" "My name is Damian." Aunjanue jumps from her bath, quickly searching for a gown rushing him out! Aunjanue falls to the floor, clinching her fist, letting out a loud eerie cry for Gods and mortals to hear from throughout the city. Drogheda appears in concern, as she consoles a weaken Aunjanue, she ask her mother, "Have I done the most unholy? No man has reached my heart the way my son has! I ask, mother please! I beg you rid me of this torment. I can't bare to live forever with this heartache! I slept with my own damn child!" Drogheda hugs her in heartache, expressing a worry, "My dear in doing so, I can't bring you back home.

You will live here and be a mortal. I want you to consider this my love." Drogheda gives her daughter six days to reconsider her decision.

Drogheda in tears, brings to her daughter a drink. Concocted from Josephine it was a potion to shorten a Gods life to the life of a mortal. Drogheda warns her daughter that the side effects will cause her to age rapidly, one of the components being hypochlorous acid, a chemical found in bleach products. Drinking the liquid, Aunjanue drops all her clothes and lives in the nude for her remaining days. The only piece of clothing she kept on was her shoulder armor. She spoke with close hybrids and invited Gods to her home. They sang and drank and ate. They stayed up into the late night gossiping. After the guest left, to her surprise, that night, Tyrothion showed up with a horse, Taneja, a reddish brown Thoroughbred. They talked for a while and kissed one last time. Before leaving, he tells her, "I know the truth of our son, I will find Damian and bring him home to live and never tell him of his mothers demise."

That morning, a crispy breeze blows through the bay window. Aunjanue begins to feel sick. The drugs begin to take affect of her body as she rubs her skin with rose hip. Aunjanue steps onto her balcony letting the sun hit her as she lights a match and prays in her mothers native tongue, a Gaelic song as she sets a flame to herself. She doesn't scream, but cries a slow tear as her ashes are blown back into her home.

"The environment was temperamental. The sunny days there felt good and within this environment, *good,* felt a little too good to be true. The dark days however, were familiar to those whose origins were born within this plain. Though the offspring of the Sun Goddess, they grew into nocturnal mortals who found the radius between four corners comforting. Some even called them, Ghetto Gods, men on the brink of ridding their families of generational curses. Bleach shirts faded from the native's wardrobe as the season progressed into a dark cloud. Their uniforms transformed into a camouflage, blending in with the dull orange and red brick homes with green and gray landscape. The rhythmic sounds of Henos footsteps harmonious with that of the mortals fast-paced lifestyle. There's a jazz there. Henos children sparring with sonnets, spoken word in a form of Rap. Some having no comprehension of their songs sung, but what was felt, was much more important.

Foreign vehicles with seats made of leather, the shade of Nero, gifted from the God Darious himself filled the streets. Wheels made of the finest elements as many women there chased the appeal and confidence of the great Goddess, Etoile." As Dryden concludes his tale to his son, Taurean's eyes lights up in excitement. "Father! This tale!? Is this environment a reachable plain!? Dryden replies, "Ah, yes, it is a place where one can go, but one must not stay long. It is a base- A maze... a low part of the sky we climb to." Only for so long, Taurean could commit to his father's words of warning. By the time his father left Taurean's garden, Taurean found his way trying to access this place of temperament.

Taurean met with Lord Lufkin near a river in the East-lands. A God who could help provide foresight as well as pursuit of an idea. "Why am I not accessing this place Lord Lufkin, tell me, I must know. No one is giving me access into their soul." Lufkin replies, "Many of the mortals that rest their minds there are de-

voted to their Gods. You would need to find someone who is either blood related to you or who is polytheistic." In his search, Taurean stumbled onto a very particular window of opportunity. Identical sisters who rivaled for beauty and power. They grew older as heirs to their father's empire. A father who was Legend amongst his neighborhood and respected by some Gods for his tactics of defending and controlling the Langston Projects. The first sister, was named Chaise, pronounced "Sha-se," a name given by her father for her sassiness throughout her youth.

Chaise always got what she wanted until her most current birthday. The youngest, Rosina, kept the neighborhood boys and girls in check if ever disrespect fell on her father's name. Because of this, their father, Lenox, decided to make Chaise's birthday a day of both daughters, since the only difference was their births milliseconds apart from 11:59pm to 12:00am.

"Hey Ro- ro- ra, rah- ro, ro.." Alex pretends to DJ scratch, Rosina interrupts, "Ro ro ro rah ruh! Ah shut the fuck up! Retarded ass! Fuck!" As his friends laugh on, Rosina brushes pass them to run into the corner store. Returning home from the corner store, she dumps packs of cigarettes out of her bag. Hearing her son's cries, she rushes into the room to soothe LaDouyon. Rocking his cradle, Rosina looks out the window to see Chaise heading inside. Chaise shouts, "Hey Roh-Roh!- Ah uh-oh, my goodness! Hey you little cutie!" Rosina cringes as Chaise kisses their dog on the mouth. "That's fucking gross!" Rosina shouts. Chaise continues her pecks as she introduces her friend, "What-t Ev-VER! This is Kate, you remember Kate!?" As Rosina looks back down at her son, she gives with a slight wave to Chaise friend, "Oh yea, hey, Kate." Hinting, she signals Kate to just wait in her bedroom. Chaise knocks on another door, she cracks it open simultaneously, "Pssh, Mom...!" As Chaise continues, her mother signals her with her index finger. "Ok, yea I'll let you go. You

tell everyone I said hello! Alright, alright… ok, alright, bye!" Teresa then ask, "What you want baby!?" "Mom, how you know I want something!?" Teresa stops in her tracks, rolling her eyes, laughing. "Mom! Mom! Ok! Ok! Look, I've been thinking about what Daddie told me, and I think I'm ready! I think my first order of business is to work with The Escobars, they have a system to clean our mon-" Teresa interrupts. "Now wait a minute, Baby Chaise, you think The Escobars hands ain't dirty! Ah-HA! You must be trippin'!" Teresa continues, "And what you think they doing!? You think they ain't killing and banging cuz they don't look like us. You catch them with the lights on, you'll see!

Them motherfuckers got a good ass PR firm, that's all ..! They whollll-' brand! *PERFECT*! In the eyes of motherfuckas like me and you! You weren't here yet, but your father-my husband, Lenox! A fucking Legend, them Escobars- or, or- them Rockefellers -or whoever you wanna rub shoulders with, never went to war with them white motherfuckers and actually won! They wanted this town, our clothes, our shoes, our hair, our babies! Shit! Even our fucking skin! They wanted all that- and your father, fought them motherfuckers with his wallet, his heart, and his integrity. What he started baby, is fine. You don't always wanna rush to work with people who don't look like you." As Teresa tries to embrace Chaise, she runs out the room and goes to grab Kate. Teary eyed Chaise lets out a squawk, "Let's go Kate!"

When bored with herself, Chaise would gallivant for joyous facial expressions from the boys at the corner store in front of the projects. "Ugh, ill Lenny! Do mommy know you still outside- Oooh! Hey cutie! I like your Threes! They cute! You should've got the same color, we could've been matching!" "Chaise can you please go home! And Taurean don't like yo ass!" Chaise wanted Taurean, not because she liked him, but simply because everyone else did. Taurean, was known for his physique, confi-

dence and charisma. He was somewhat of an intellect and carried a demeanor where most men feared him, and all women respected him. Out of favor for Lenny, Taurean kept quarrels with rivals in town against Lenny's father at bay. In his favor, Lenny was protected by Taurean's aura. A Gods aura was much more different than that of any mortals or Legend or Icon. This Aura was not necessarily better, but different. An aura with an aroma of foundation, forever consistency and continuous habit of playfulness.

"Thanks! Yea, they came out a few days ago," Taurean responding to Chaise. Chaise smirks and walks off with her friend as Lenny looks at Taurean with a possum smile. Lenny, laughing it off, "Mannn, she doin' way too much!" Lenny and his friends were the neighborhoods sundials, pivoting in front of the store for hours until sunset. Taurean, fixing his sneakers, hears a tire peel in the distance. "Pick ya head up," Taurean, speaking to everyone but looking at Lenny. Lenny's entourage circles him in his defense. A car peels out of the darkness as the passenger shoots at the corner. Everyone drops to the floor, meanwhile, Taurean pretends to react to the gun shots, throwing himself to the ground. Laying there, he contemplates if this charade of mortal fear is beneficial in the long run. Taurean gets up, wiping his sneakers of any scuff marks, as neighbors shout out of the window in panic.

Teresa comes down from their apartment shouting in tears as Rosina carrying her son, walks across the street cursing Lenny with a rebuttals, "Bitch! Fuck you! You think you tough! You ain't tough!" Rosina looks at their mother, "I know you hear him right!? You better fucking get him Mommy!" Teresa tries to mend the tension but, Rosina continues, "Just give him a bottle, he'll be 'ight... fucking alcke'! You *niggerstupid*! You gonna fuck around and get yo ass shot thinking you Daddy!" Lenny hears this and pucks himself onto a crate. Fingers interlocked; he buries his head into his palms taking his time to speak. "Look man, I don't know who shot

at us, Ok! All I know is they got a *blueasscar* and aint no nigga over here got no blue-ass-car. So I know it was them niggas from the Eastside!" Taurean interjects calmly, "Hey, ah, pardon me, Imma get outta here, ya make sure ya get home soon, I can hear the sirens coming- and ladies ya have a goodnight." Taurean walks off to the back of the projects.

Rosina notice Taurean walking up the block and then quickly doubling back to their project building. She sees a man talking to him. He was taller than anyone she knew, and his voice was dominant. "This isn't a game; you need to find it before it's too late. I've said this to you for years, this place is a maze and you must keep a distance from the mortals! Do not interfere! Haven't you learn many lessons like this in the past!? This environment is not what you think, if not careful son, you may be stuck here forever." Rosina, hiding in between two cars couldn't quite see the man's face, but only caught a glimpse of his beard. A loud noise distracts Rosina and by time she peaks back to see who Taurean was speaking to, they both are gone.

Lenny grew closer to Taurean after the shootout, making him a top chief in the projects. Taurean spent most of his mornings in the park and playground. He worked a lot on his arms and chest, utilizing the monkey bars as gym equipment while listening to music on a large speaker. Though it was affecting his stamina, after working out, he would often find himself eating a ton of Chinese food at a restaurant where they sold bootleg karate films. It was here, Taurean realized some of the Nero mortals, worshiped Asian deities. Rosina would catch him there in the early afternoon, usually to walk back with him to the corner where Lenny and his friends would congregate.

Chaise walks up with her friend, as she sees Rosina is talking to Taurean while Lenny friends shoot dice. "You always want what I have! Oh my God! Please find your own man!" Rosina turns rolling her eyes, "Yea whateva-

yea, Kate! Hey-or whatever. You know what!? Chaise, let me have a word with you." Rosina pauses and then shouts, "You know what!? Fuck that! Stop bringing these motherfuckers around! You sponsorin' her hood-visa or something! They sit out here with all that *hehe* shit with cats from the hood until that *Nigga* come out and then they hollerin' *I'm scared, I'm scared!*"

As Rosina continues her rant, her brother, and Taurean laugh a bit as Kate starts to get uncomfortable. Lenny replies, "Come on man, let her be." Rosina shouts, "Yeah! You say that shit now until she got Johnny-law on yo ass. You know why I'm hot Chaise!? Cuz you always bringing her into our shit! I don't even know where you live Kate. Like, where the fuck are you even from!? Oh, now you can't talk! You motherfuckers know everyone language but ours!" Chaise shouts, "Ok, Rosina chill!" She blocks her sister from approaching Kate. Taurean puts his arm around Rosina, massaging her left shoulder. "Come on let's take a walk- clear the air for a bit." A fueled Rosina continues, "I can't fucking stand her ass! Just hanging around soaking up shit, like bitch! What the fuck are you even doing here! Haha ha!"

Rosina vent concludes after Taurean hands her a cup of tea from the café a few blocks away. "Mm, this is good, thank you. Yea there's a lot funny shit out here I'm ready to just leave this place." Taurean responds, "Leave! You clearly have enough means." "And go where!?" Rosina replied. "It ain't a matter of money to me, what matters is the family. I want to go somewhere and there's family, you know! My father left me in charge, even over my *older* sister. I mean you know about his empire at this point, but what got him started was the phony money. Them' dead presidents kept us afloat when that drought came. Only Washingtons too…! Nothing too crazy, he flipped them shits until we were *gucci*. But my high-yella ass sister wants to be *Big-Willy* and deal with The Escobars. They control the Eastside and know how to create larger bills at a faster rate, plus

have a strong relationship with Po-Po. So I'm here, to make sure the family do right by our father and make better decisions, you feel me!?" Taurean observes the martyr complex creep into the mind of Rosina. Sitting on a top of a bench with her arms wrapped around both her knees still upset. Taurean had no clue of what made her snappy with her sisters' friend. "Maybe she didn't like the idea of Kate being around me," a thought that pondered Taurean's mind. "Let's get something to drink!" Rosina repeated. "You just had tea and water and juice." "No Taurean, I want an adult drink! Hahaha!" Sucking his teeth, Taurean decided to accompany Rosina. Forcing Taurean a sip from her bottle, he playfully dodges her attempts to pour some into his mouth. "Why don't you drink," Taurean steps back, replying, "It's just not my thing." Rosina takes a sip from the cap, mimicking, "Drugs just aunt' my thing! Hahaha! Oh, so you be frontin'! You stay with a blunt behind your ear. You know what!? Damian was the same way- No! No! I don't drink! Imma God! Ahhh!"

"Where is he now, your sons' father?" Rosina replies, "I'm not sure, last time I spoke to him he told me he was on some journey for some guy named He-ro or Heknou, something like that- shit, when I'm drunk, I be forgetting what you say anyhow!" An opportunistic Taurean favors Rosina misfortune. With a slight smile, "My real name is Taurh, I am a God, I am here for my love of this place, and you, if I'm being honest. Your son is my grandson. The reason I cannot drink is based on a paradoxical theory that if we Gods take drugs, we may fall into a mortal-like addictive state or simply die. If a God dies from mortal potions, they were in fact, an actual God, but to fall into an addiction, is to suggest we were never a God to begin with. No one knows for sure, so us Gods do not wager our immortal life for an unsure one. And the man you speak of is Henos, he is a son to my Aunt. Rosina stares dead into the eyes of Taurean, and then lets out a burst of laughter, following her liquor bottle dropping out

her hand, "Ah-ha! Nigga whatever! Walk me home man, it's getting cold!" A slurred and off balanced Rosina speaks, "Soooo… tell me more about your world! Like whose here and why I don't see them and shit- How come I see you!?" Taurean examples, "Well it's simple, one, I choose to be seen, but you will never see a God in true form. Many Gods are here. You see that car over there? It was made in the Spirit of Ecstasy. To Gods, we know of her as Eleanor, and she favors the feeling of immense emotion. My son, Damian, he is also a great leader and God. Even Henos children are here, deities of music and language." As they stop in front of a theater, Rosina replies in shock, "Who?" Rosina looking up at the marquee. "Wait! What! Word!? Apollo! Yo! That's wild crazy! Uptown cats love Apollo! Ha-ha! Apollo out here with jungle fever!"

Rosina's laugh ends abruptly, "Grandpa, You think they pray to you too? Taurean responds, "I'm not sure? I don't feel their call. A sure way to know who a mortal prays is to inspect what charm they are wearing" Rosina laughing, "Ok, what the hell is a charm, like a lucky charm!?" "Oh boy! No, not a lucky charm," Taurean follows with a chuckle. "A totem or charm. We all carry them. A symbol to mortals that tells you who they pray to. For us Gods it is a way to transport. Multiple charms can be used to cast spells or enchantments. I'll tell you more next time you decide to have one of these Weogufka enchantments!"

Rosina walking into the elevator turns around to him, "Weo who!?" Taurean places his hands over his face and laughs. Taurean heading back to the blocks, spots Lenny, seeing him unsettled. "Hey what's up with you brother!? Word around is you messing with my sister!" A confused Taurean insist Lenny does not understand the dynamic between Rosina and him. "Look! Stop fucking with my sister's, before shit get crazy for you!" As Taurean sees a misguided Lenny, he tries to avoid a conflict, Taurean,

steps away, walking away calmly, also, taking with him, his *favor* for Lenny. Taurean's therapy for conflict usually followed with eating or shopping. One permanent trend he followed of the Nero was use of black silhouettes with the help of the Gods tailor, Darious. A God the Nero mostly prayed to in this land. He was a God of true craftsmanship and precision. He favored the mortal who appreciated quality and time. His son, Trin; by locals, Trem', was their primary tailor when Darious was not around. Darious built a reputation by blending ancient African and Greek garments. Some of the fabric worked as armor for civilians or Tribesmen. Safeguards were created within these garments to fight against psychological enchantments or charms such as self-deprecation, low self-esteem, and even heartache.

Taurean felt drawn to boast throughout the streets in his new wardrobe. Normally avoiding certain areas, he decided to travel into them, in search of mortal validation. Brushing his hair, Taurean looks down at his new gold Rolex watch with a modified band made of cowrie shells which complimented his draped sable-colored pant with loafers that embellishing cowrie shells over the tongue. "Excuse me," an older lady walking past him as he stands in front of a museum, "Can you tell me the time young man?" He chuckles in response, "I don't wear it to check the time, the streetlights lets me know when it's getting dark." Arriving back to the projects, Taurean hears that very same squeaky car sound again. Knowing what's to follow, moving at a Godspeed back to Lenny, he is still too late to avoid the inevitable. As gunshots flare, Lenny is shot several times, dropping to the floor. Taurean props Lenny head up trying to observe his body to see if the gunshots were fatal. Lenny coughing up blood, barely getting a word out, "You… you did- Did this…" Police sirens wane towards them, as Taurean leaves Lenny laying semiconscious as he makes a run for it. Looking to the skies, he sees a dark cast of a quiet storm moving in. A

sign his father once mentioned. "I could of swore I came this way already," a panicked Taurean says aloud to himself. Overwhelmed, he becomes entrenched, circling the projects becoming more lost. In a matter of seconds, the sky turns to a dark purple hue, as the ground hides beneath a blanket of snow. He sits down near the playground fatigued. In his moments of despair, he calls on his father yet again. "I have failed you; I have failed myself. I neglected my diet. With lack of nourishment, the food here leaves me with an everlasting hunger. I have neglected my spirituality. I have not prayed often since I found worldly things as a substitute for my core stability. I call to you to give me strength to resist the indulgence of mortal temptations. I am exhausted, constantly moving through this world and this community to not just live, but survive."

Sometime after his prayer, Taurean hears a distinctive call, a sound similar to a bone tapped against metal traveling in the wind. Those who heard this call, knew the call of Orizah. The Goddess of Nourishment was sent to Taurean. He followed the sound. He arrived to a vacant alley with frozen dirt. There laid a shovel. A voice called to him and said, "Dig! Dig into your culture, dig for your identity! There are many unfamiliar who dig into our community for resources. Remember why your soil is important." As Taurean took heed, he dug for hours and seeds arranged in several baskets. It was here, Taurean was gifted with the blessing of intention and growth. Using a tarp to build moisture and nurture the plants for some months. Sprouting out of the soil was potatoes, rice, carrots, oranges, and melons. Taurean kept his promise to maintain a healthier diet. His garden began to expand causing natives to form a weekly visit to his potager.

He couldn't believe it, such nourishment was neglected from the neighborhood. Only processed foods and liquor and spirits was fuel for the locals. One sunny day, he sees a young woman walking his direction with a child, holding an ice cream in his hand. "Hey how have you been?" Rosina heard of his garden from a teacher at her sons school. She replies, "I've been good. You know I'm mad at you!" She laughs a bit. "You left my brother to die. He ina wheelchair now man! Where the hell have you been!?" Taurean arranging bags tells his helper to finish up while gesturing to walk with Rosina. "A lot has happen on both sides, I pray he finds peace and understanding. But I seen Magn- I mean, police rush. And I couldn't afford to get caught. When I was with him, he was always protected I made sure of that." Rosina replies, "Yea, my brother was an idiot anyway, I told him he gonna get his ass shot one day. It is what it is, ya feel me. But one thing I'm upset with is my stupid ass sister! She learned her lesson too! Ended up getting locked up after the Escobars used her as a scapegoat for some scam shit.

Rosina, finding closure, rushes into give Taurean a hug. "Thank you Grandpa!" Taurean looks down stunned, "Wait, what!? How do you-" Rosina laughs, "I wanted to know who you really were. You took advantage of that moment thinking I would forget, I never forget, regardless, if I'm drunk or not! I even got a charm made for your grandson it needs your blessing." Taurean not sure whether to be shocked or excited, responds, "Wow, I can't believe it, we are told never to reveal the truth to mortals." Rosina releases from her hug, looking up at Taurean, "Yea that's cute and all, but Grandpa, I got one thing I need to say... Stop saying you like me! That's some white shit!" They both laugh, as Taurean picks up Ladouyon and walks back into the garden.

Many of the towns took a hard hit, Calabria especially. Nike took issue and sought punishment for the lack of praise the locals had for her.
At the time, the natives felt more scared of the backlash from Mus-
solini. During the war, Nike went to battle for her remaining followers, mainly stationed in Naples. Many soldiers became ill and injured,
and many believers of hers died. She decided to plan an exit strategy.

Guiding her army out of the land, she sees two jets flying overhead, one
appearing to be American aircraft and second German. The American pi-
lot maneuvers, avoiding bullets shot from the other jet fighter. The co-pilot
shouts through his headset, "James we got 2 on us at 7o'clock! They're hot!"
Slipping through a stream of clouds, James' wing is then hit, sending them
in a free fall. Shot out of the sky, the jet crash lands on the outskirts of the
town. Nike and a few of her soldiers trail up the hill to see if there were any
survivors. Going up in smoke, Bill drags his partner James from the man-
gled jet, the radio frequency is damaged as they try to make contact with a
friendly fire jet. Bill manages to get to cover in a home that was mostly demolished. James, with a broken hip and dislocated arm, tries to convince Bill
to get out of there. Determined, he breaks open an adrenaline pack to give
to James. While staying low, they overhear a German voice approaching.

Within a couple hours, Nike arrived up the hill, seeing the two Americans
are still alive, surviving off small rations of water and a chocolate bar. All the
while, a group of Germans move in closer. Catching Bill and James in a vulnerable location, the Germans point their guns at Bill intensely yelling and
sliding James out of the buildings debris across the jagged tar. Bill is asked
to draw out any weapons that he or James may have. Nike observes how Bill
managed to stay alive yet showed a willingness to die for a fellow man. Nike
waits to intervene as she notices the man negotiates with the two soldiers.
Bill stands up, facing the Germans as they shout more erratic. Un-

aware of what they're saying, but their tone suggested death as Bill looks on trying not to make a sudden move. He looked at them shouting, "Just take me! Send him home alive! He has a family! He's hurt!"

One of the soldiers spoke several languages, asking Bill why the sacrifice. Bill tells the man, "A necessary sacrifice for one of us to live over two of us dead." The bilingual soldier looks at his team and waves his hand over their guns to drop them. He hands Bill water and tells him, "Leave! Simple! Yea!? Plain! This is not your fight!" Nike in the distance watching, noticed a young handsome man, strong arms and hard chest. He carried himself as a very sure man. Bill hears a whisper. A voice calls to him, "You are safe." In fear, Bill ask, "Who is there!?" Bill looks around putting up a stick, shouting again, "Who are you!? Who is there!" Nike speaks louder, "You know in your heart I am here and I come not to harm you." Nike approaches Bill. She was a soldier, built like an Amazonian woman with a wingspan that of a vulture with a shield with a womens face on it. A spear made of marble and a dagger that never left her right hand. Nike wanted to offer Bill favor. She gives Bill a role of animal skin, "Here, this area gets a bit breezy during night fall." Along with cloth, she hands him piece of her armor. Nike speaks briefly, "I saw your soul, you show compassion and possess a all-or-nothing mindset. This spirit will do me well. I need to leave and I need you to bring me to your land. I wager there will be believers like yourself there." As Nike continues, "I can provide you protection and strategy and stability. You will have the gift of insight and the ability to be victorious with very little effort."

What Nike wanted was to eventually step away from the shadow of Zeus. As she explains, "I lived as a high general for the Olympian Zeus, but I see these lands are dying of true believers and for that, I will not last long as well. For centuries I sat at the side of Athena as their general and strategist for Zeus. Though it was not easy, somehow, I remained praised by

mortals here on earth. In my journey, I waited centuries for this opportunity. I believe you are my way into a new world." Bill seemed excited, not because of her offer and blessing, but the fact that Gods existed. Without any hesitation, Bill accepts Nike offer. In a burst, "Wow! I never thought there was a female God, he says as he kneels in praise." He waited under the demolished house with his partner James until that next morning when they were rescued by their search party.

Bill made his way stateside, stepping away from the army for a bit. He spent time working on a farm and working as a coach at the nearby High school. Most of the coaching involved training runners and long jumpers. The students were dedicated and talented; however, they failed to secure any victories for the school. Most of their shoes would rip from the rubber lining inside the shoes within two to three long jumps and the first couple of laps. He looks at a shoe that broke off from a student and shouts in anger, "Fuck! At this rate, we won't have any shoes left in town!" Bill did not hear from Nike since he arrived home. Frustrated, he decided to pray to her. He hears a voice in his head, "Tough skin". Then it hits him. Bill runs to go get the roll of leather Nike gave him to use as warmth in overseas. Over the next few weeks, he had running shoes lined with strips of the leather Nike had given him. The lining alternated to leather improved the marriage between the shoe and the sole, preventing it from ripping apart.

During his training with the student-athletes, Bill wanted to test out some of his tailored shoes on this track. One runner, started out, though the shoes were slightly tighter, they also gave a better grip from, foot-to-pavement. The runner breezes around the lap, then Bill clicks his timer. Not only did the shoes hold intact, but they shaved almost 20 seconds off their lap time. As Bills shoes began to take off as a success for the student-athletes, the high school grew an interest in investing in Bill's shoes from a business

aspect to fund the schools' sports desires. Locals showed up to Bills home on weekends asking to purchase some shoes for the sake of jogging or recreational activities. As business began to boom, Bill heard a voice again, it was Nike coming to Bill. On a charcoal gray afternoon, she wanted to see how he's been going along. She smiles, "I see the leather has been helpful!". Bill praises her continuously, as he ask for more. Without a complaint, Nike hands him fabric and ask what is his plan for the shoes. As he explains, she grants him a small touch on his shoulder and disappears. The days pass, Bill starts to talk around town in finding people to help build his shoe empire. After a week or so, he meets with a businessman that was known around town for bringing small businesses into a larger market.

They hit it off instantly, sitting and talking for hours. The conversation itself was mainly about the crappy coffee in town, cattle and agriculture. As they concluded, Phil, became a business partner with Bill to grow the brand and find manufactures to produce more sneakers. Standing up to leave the diner, Phil asks, "So what's the name of the brand going to be called?" Bill paused for a moment creating anticipation, "I named it Blue Star, but after some consideration I'm calling it *Nike*". They stood up to shake hands and see each other off.

Nike popularity increased in Bill's hometown. In a few months, it grew over to the nearby cities and states. This popularity of the shoe brand began to give notice to Goddess, Nike. As Bill worked to build Nike, he receives a letter from Aeoris, a loyal bird sent from the God, Potis. Aeoris is usually sent to oversee and extract and deliver messages to Potis. The letter requested Bill arrange the arrival of Potis to come to see him for an important mission. Bill awaiting his arrival, standing in a sweet corn field with an Axe with a charm the shape of a pyramid, he shouts, "One country, One flag, One language!" Bill throws the charm to the

ground and chopping the Axe into it. The sky turns to a deep smoked charcoal pulling firey lighting in from mountains. A small pocket of white light is seen from above, as heavy winds blow Bill from behind.

Suddenly, a large foot is seen stepping from the sky. An oversize palm, then a long droopy face with a wide jaw. Bill is now standing in front of the God of Supremacy. Potis often carried a poker face, showing little to no body language and barely wore clothes or weapons for that matter. He looks on to Bill and speaks, "I am here and I ask for your loyalty yet again. I see you've brought a Goddess into my domain Bill." Potis then looks up to the skies, making a screeching noise. This sound was a call that brought Nike to appear. Potis looks upon Nike and explains, "I understand you convinced a child of mine to bring you here, but this is my land, my domain. No man or God lives rent free. Your stay here owes a debt!" As Potis steps forward to Nike, he explains to her that there can be a peaceful compromise. "I understand you are a Goddess of Victory, I demand victory and with your assistance, I shall have it!" Poised Nike gathers her thoughts before speaking, "You remind me of *him*, the great Olympian, Zeus. He was powerful in his words and mighty in his actions. Potis ego was stroked as Nike continues, "I have heard about you for some time, you force your power onto your believers, you are God of Supremacy, God of Entitlement and Privilege. That being said, you practice no awareness." As Nike draws her dagger, approaching Potis. "As a guest in your home, I offer my services willingly. I see the potentials in us working together instead of separate. As payment, I can offer you insight to any domestic conflict you may have."

As Nike and Potis agree, Potis ask Nike to investigate a potential war between the Elbrus and Nero conflict. What Nike was able to provide was a structural and strategic plan to hinder most of the Nero mortals from overpowering Elbrus mortals. However, during the Civil Rights wars, Nike no-

ticed something disturbing about Potis tactics. Meeting with him in a state of anger she explains, "I now see what drives you, at first I thought it was to obtain power. No man, no women, should suffer what you demonstrated in battle. Raping and slaughtering men and women was not part of the plan."

Potis with a sinister laugh, "It's necessary obsession! How do you think they arrived to these lands!? You think they were asked! No! They were forced!" Nike looks on in disappointment and expresses her interest to remain neutral in the quarrel between Potis and the Nero. Potis upset of Nike's decision, threatens to remove Nike from the new land. Nike spreads her wings, trapping him into her wingspan, "You're in no position to question or ridicule my decision. Your blind focus to rid those of their race will ruin your empire. When I worked close to Athena, she taught me a few things. One thing I learned is you win when your enemies are closest to you. You can watch every habit and ritual they make. When you rid the world of your enemy the only enemy is yourself." This wedge Potis created between him and Nike led to their mortal followers having discourse with the other's followers.

As Nike wanted to focus more on her *American Dream*, sports and fashion was becoming a dominant spirit in culture of America. As Bill worked on recruiting athletes, she noticed they could not quite win over in sports including basketball, sprint and tennis. She seen an opportunity here. Nike searched for the specific athletes. She decided to change her appearance, resembling that of a Nero woman. This was also a strategy she brought to Drogheda and her offspring in their personal pursuits. She arrived in a small town to spectate at a local athletic training center within the Southlands. She called herself *Ignacia*. A defined, muscular young woman, red undertones and peachy cheeks. She had the physique of an Olympic swimmer. Within moments of her arrival, she encounters multiple athletes, all tall in stature and excellent in their chosen field.

Standing on the sidelines, she is approached by a man. A towering dark-skinned man the shade of a blueberry. He carried a strong accent, that of Geechee natives. Offering Ignacia a seat, he speaks, "Hey, how you doin' hunnie? Dose sum nice shoes you have on". She didn't really speak, she just presented a certain demeanor where she wasn't approachable. "Deya call me *Cooter* round these yads. I, Captain of this ship they call Helena! Yo tell me yo name!?" As Ignacia looks confused, "I'm sorry I'm trying to watch this game, I can't quite understand you!" Waiting for a reply, jokingly Cooter responds, "Aha yea, yu frum Texas! Gotdamnit, I knuw it! Looka here child, you got that eye on this game or the playas, if watchin' dem, you come with me to our festival tonight, I can have you meet with the playas!"

Ignacia smiles figuring this would be her way in. She arrives in an un-usual outfit as Cooter comments, "Shum ther red cloth, are you fight-ing for a bull!? Ha-ha!" Ignacia looks on with a stunned looked on her face. Inspecting the guest, she was aware the members of the Geechee people wore indigo dyed gowns and pants. Such custom was prac-ticed with the enslaved, working on cotton plantations dying fabrics.

As they enter the festival, Cooter pulls Ignacia back from approaching the athletes, "Hey, we raise up here different honnie, we dance, we laugh you know first! We talk'em up, then talk'em into your pleasures last, you will see dem soon but for right now you groove with me to a dance!" As they dance, Cooter sways from side to side, moving his hands from his waist to the air. The music played was from Ayeles and Kalimbas and sticks knocked against wash boards. Steel pans, drums and French horns as the native Gullah women sing . He notices Ignacia having a hard time keeping up. "Hey girl, whatcha deal, swing with me!" The beat of the music picks up all the while Ignacia loses her focus on the dance and keeping her eye on the players in which she seen at the gym earlier. Cooter slows down, grabbing Ignacia at

the waist, "Hey you'd mind we step way from here?" As they exiting the dance floor, Cooter replies with a laugh, "Now where'd you say you wer fum!?"

Ignacia looks at him confused and responds, "I'm sorry, I don't know what you mean". "Ol, lil' lady cut the shit! I know you'd not who you say you are! You say youah a scout! You say you fum the Soufh! All those may be true but you know what gave it away!? Your lack of our language! Your attire and more directly! Lack to keep up with the beat of our music! Cooter laughs grows into anger!, "Your lack of understanding, your color of your skin does not make you Nero, yu ahlso need intangibles!" As Cooter forces Ignacia outside, she is unknowingly surrounded by his Tribe members. Ignacia looks around, reaching behind her back for a dagger she kept hidden. Before she could draw her weapon, Cooters Tribes all point guns and swords at her neck. As Ignacia transforms returns to her normal state. Seeing her true form, Cooter walks in front of his men, blocking them from attacking Nike. "Now this lil' lady think cuz she Nike we folk down here don't fear of a lil' scuffle or killin'! God or not, you can face penalty for such action. Ha! Portraying Nero by sight and not by soul!"

He waves them back as he transforms. Standing in from of his men blocking their view from a shot, Cooter evolves into his true form, Droger. Droger was a quick thinker and he favored those who took risk. He was somewhat taller than most Gods. Droger held an exaggerated nostril and little to know facial hair. He spent time around and sometimes trained with athletes but wasn't limited to just sports enthusiast. Droger, God of Perseverance, Risk, Flight and Forwardness, which meant he loved innovation and dream builders. He adored risk takers and hated depression or idleness. Droger would personally assist in a mortals project or idea giving them an advantage even if it seemed scientifically impossible. As Nike is threatened to explain her agenda she replies. "I've been in contact

with Drogheda's children that you were the person to see about working with the greatest sportsmen in the lands. My actions are my fault alone, I should have asked permissions of Gods as yourself but I was left to take a risk due to the fact there are no leaders in your Tribe that came forth."

Nike pleads to Droger for a pardon and discusses she needs the best athletes to compete against her Olympians back home such as Zeus and Athena. If she is worthy of a win, her name shall stand alone. "During the time I spent overseas, I've watched many Nero mortals possess true greatness in their sport. These Nero will me an advantage in physical and contact sports." Droger replies, "I thought you guys love the big brute humans, Piruphius is a fan of physique and a lot of his believers share his similar stature." Nike replying with certainty, "Yes I have reached out to him, but his believers somewhat intimidate the games opponent to the point of an unfair match. The games are meant to win with such finesse and entertainment. Though his men are strong and brute, that does not certify the makings of an athlete, for they are warriors."

Droger with a slick smirk, "Are yo people unsame!? A mess full of things I swear. I do not wish to quarrel! Enough! I am looking for a solution here. What is your proposition!?" Nike offering a compromise, "In return for your help and athletes, I will grant you protection from Magnus and his offspring and the ability for your name to grow beyond these walls of America. I understand from your followers, their conflict is finance. They shall have no worry in that matter. "All things considered, the one thing you can't guarantee is the athletes loyalty!" Droger continues, "Let's make this fun! Theres nothin' you can grant me that I cant grant myself. How bout we make a wager!?" Nike, a competitive sport, agrees. They will indulge in the lives of three athletes seeing if the majority chooses to praise to Nike or Droger. The loser will forfeit

their God status and immortality. Droger, shook on this with confidence. Droger decides to introduce Nike to a number of his potential champions. "Yu see ther!? Been watching these jukes since before dey in human form. I watched their souls when their fathers and mothers were young." The first player Nike chose was a racket player. She favored her due to her built of the Amazon women, close to Queen Hippolyta. Her golden-brown skin tone was a great advantage when players sparred in the days of hot sun along with her gift arm reach. Nike was impressed with Serena. She was trained since young and held great discipline. The second, was a "Road-Runner". She was rumored to be the fastest and most experienced sprinter, long jumper and endurance runner.

Nike needed one more player. She overheard an athlete constantly chatting up to his opponent on the court. She walked past him to observe his demeanor. She despised his arrogance but couldn't take her eyes off him. A mortal, that can leap beyond others limitations. Elongated libs and arms and agile ability; he played with such grace. Droger spoke, "Whatcha mind make of him!?" Nike paused for a moment to process her thought. "He possesses an opinionated persona. To learn, requires two ears and no mouth. He will have no ears and all mouth. His place as a athlete may fall second to his place of speech. This may deter my future athletes to be in league with me. Nonetheless, I am desperate, so I shall take him, flaws and all." The training wasn't simple, Nike and Droger invested time in these athletes daily, planning diets and training routines and facilities for the athletes. Droger involvement with the mortals was exploring their true passions and drives. If a mortal who praised him wanted to jump higher, Droger simply would bless them with stronger cartilage in their knee, providing them with support with turbulence in general. Droger would often say, "Because how can my believer jump higher if there is nothing to support his landing!" Most days, athletes spent

ten to fifteen hours straight training. Nike's opinionated Michael would spend about fifteen to twenty hour practicing before even sweating.

Droger brought the God of Unity, Piruphius to the games to watch Michael and the others play. Piruphius loved the games. He was a fan of mortal athletes. The idea to him was glorious, watching opponents compete without the end result of death. He would attend some games at times as a spectator or sometimes change himself to an official referee within the matches.

Brought to Droger attention from Piruphius, he suggested approaching Nike about replacing the basketball player Michael for a player of interest, Lynn. Nike declined, feeling that Michael was more well versed and best suited. During there debate, Piruphius suggests a better way to solve the disagreement is to simply have the two players fight for their spot. One night before the match, Darious, the wise and favorable craftsmen for Gods and mortals, is met by a *God*. Darious made use of preowned fabrics from Greek Gods or foreign warriors outfits. He reused the fabric with Nero cotton. These new garments were commissioned by mortals and Gods as a armor for protection, giving the buyer a great deal of confidence and self-esteem. Darious greeting *Piruphius*, is interrupted- "I want to make a contribution to one of my praised believers, an athlete, he has earned a gift of incentive." Darious moving pretty quickly, gathers notes and references for this unique offering. Darious asks, "When would you need this by, Lord Piruphius!?" He speaks low toned, "Immediately- in a few days! And what is your fee for such service!?" Darious looks in confusion. Impatient Piruphius walking away, "Ah, nevertheless, we shall settle up when I return!" In two days time, the shoes were gifted as a perk for future praise from the athlete. Sneakers with the finest cow hide, and oil used as lubrication for insole. Darious attached vulture wings, retrieved from the mid-west; attaching them to the ends of the shoe. Prior to the game, Droger standing on the side-

line noticing the shoes Michael has on. Nervously looking over to Piruphius, Droger questions, "How in the hell can this be!? A trick has been made on us!" Michael, now with an added advantage, took control of the match. Droger, seeing the potential slaughter, calls to Lynn, telling to stay close to Michael and not to let me elevate over him during the game. In doing so, Michael lost one of his shoes from roughness during the game. As the game progressed, the two players bickered over the issue of too much body contact. Michael thrived off this chaos, making him channel his focus. He began to get into Lynn's head. Michael palming the ball over Lynn's head taunts him, "You not a ballplayer! Yousa' crackhead!" He takes one step towards the right then left of Lynn; spinning off him, breezing pass him, he takes two large steps from the three-point line and finally leaping over the foul line, winning the game.

Battered and bruised both athletes shake hands and walk over to the bench to rest. Michael looks down at his shoes, "Man! You dogged my shoes man, ha haha!" Lynn replies, "Yea, those are fly man where you get them from. "Oh, uhh, it was a gift from Nike man, they fuck with me over there". Overhearing this, a perplexed Piruphius looks to Droger and responds, "I am heading to go see Darious!" Upon greeting him, Darious asks, "I take it the Olympian was pleased with the shoes?" Darious somewhat off put, tries to jog Piruphius memory, "You came in the other day with an illustration of shoes you wanted. You continued to say, *we have Nike worried, and this will eliminate her from the wager between her and Droger.*" Piruphius distraught, pauses for a second, "Your Greatness! You're telling me you believed Nike to be *me*!? Was there no other sign to give you certainty and authenticity!?" Darious upset with himself, "I do believe what was odd to me was your-I mean, *her*, offer of money for my services. Money for art can exhaust the creative process." An upset Piruphius knocks down a large mirror and leaves, heading back to Droger. Nike did not introduce Lynn to drugs directly, but knew his weakness for

it after hearing about it during the ball game. Nike feared Lynn, though not a fan, would be drafted into the basketball league, right along Michael potentially surpassing her chosen one. Josephine, Goddess of Herb and Medicine, was primary during this era in the lives of the Nero of America. Her purpose was to heal Gods and Goddess of immortal wounds. Mortals themselves, were influenced by her compounds from her son, Weogufka. He was responsible for sneaking into her potions and liquids and plants and creating new concoctions. These agents were powerful to Gods but deadly to humans. Gods cannot take toxins solely created for humans. In doing so, it will eventually turn them human or into a ghost instead of a God.

During the draft into the league, Lynn and his friends sought out party favors to celebrate, assuming Lynn's guaranteed spot as a professional ball player. Weogufka, was a pusher, often misusing his mothers compounds by sharing them with mortals. Anticipating Josephine's son habits, Nike added a compound into Josephine's drugs. With the correct dose for a God, these compounds are meant to add clarity and consistency, but taken by a mortal, this would be fatal. Lynn sat on the edge of his seat watching the television awaiting the call that will change his life and the life of his family. His friend pours out a new line of coke, enticing Lynn, "Come on bro! We got one bump left!" Looking down at the table, Lynn draws an intense pull through his nostrils pulling everything from debris to lint off the glass through a rolled up dollar bill. Lynn sits back as his blood rushes to his brain. As he relaxes for a few seconds, the announcer confirms through the television. "And yes! And here you have it Lynn! Second pick for the Boston Celtics! You can hear his fans cheer on!" The crowd applauds as the head coach and owner celebrate their decision. The phone begins to ring. Stops, and then repeats again. Eric, Lynn's friend jumps up excited, "Yo! Bro we fucking made it!" As he looks over to see Lynn eyes wide open somewhat slumped

down the couch. Finding out about Lynn's death, Droger and Piruphius both approach Nike as she greets them with a strong look of cockiness. Piruphius demanding answers, "Why would you go behind my back? Why would you deceive Darious? One of our mortals are now dead, a rule you have broken!"

Nike speaks passionately, "These are the casualties of war Piruphius. You of all should be understanding. This is a battle for immortality and status. This is a battle for glory. This match doesn't start on the field." Droger looks upon her with not a word to say. As Piruphius rages on, Droger looks in silence and non-verbally suggests to Piruphius, "Let it go." Droger fell into a bittersweet enjoyment towards the players, especially Michael. In national arenas, he exiled beyond his peers and expectations of his coaches. While in game play, Michael frequently wore his winged shoes in the games. Due to the officials restrictions, he had to restrain from his ability of flight. *His Airness*, the Gods bestowed this name to him, as he was one of the few humans who could actually fly. There was a point were all grew bored of his victories. What made Michael so great wasn't his ability to win, but ability to entertain. Michael was the chosen one. Being a mortal of high status to determine which God his fans will select. The Olympics were approaching and so was the deadline to seal the deal on players to commit to their chosen God. Athletes wore Nike's logo throughout the games, social gatherings and leisure. Their homes and the homes of their friends and family expanded the brands agenda with wearing Nike's charm. Droger approached Michael one day asking him out right, "Who do you draw your strength from?" Michael replied, "Me! Whatever is done to help me along the way is just an addition to my gift I've worked hard to achieve!" Nike wanted her athletes that were seen on televised games to remain exclusively in Nike gear and armor. As the athletes success increased, so did their egos. The athletes brought foreign cars and wore embellished armor and jewelry from Gods of Nero. As a warning, Nike cast a spell of interference on Michael's career. Ru-

mors of his gambling became public. This jealous action inflicted upon Michael, set the tone for strict compliance amongst the players. The Olympics began to take place, as connoisseurs, enthusiasts, and critics occupied the arena. Serena, the tennis player, wasn't just a dominate player on the turf. Her physique, structure and demeanor, intimidated most of her players before they even came to greet. Serena was favored by most Gods based on her personality alone. During the tournament, she faced some challenges but with the blessing of Nero Gods, and envy by Elbrus Gods, Serena showed an ability to persevere.

Finishing with an Olympic Gold medal, Serena appears in front of the media for her congratulations speech. "I just want to say thank you Nike for the support. But I have to give a huge thanks to my family back home, my people, my love ones, my father and to non other than God!" As fans watch, Droger feels a surge of energy from Serena, gaining praise from her spirit. The following days resulted in America winning over Germany and Soviet Union in the 4 x 100km. Joyner winning with the Gold, she arrives into the pit to give a speech. "First and for most, I want to thank Nike, without you, I would not be here!" As Joyner concludes, she snugs her Nike hat on tighter and walks off to rejoice with her team. Droger and Nike were now tied. The final decision fell on the punished Michael. Michael, with swag and grace, helps his team win the Olympic Gold medal! They celebrated with champagne and hugs, as Michael is brought in front for his media speech. Exhausted Michael speaks, "I mean, you know! I just go out there and give my two hundred and thirty percent every game! They gave what they could and we gave what we had!" The crowd screams as he responds to the journalist, "Well yea, Nike has definitely helped, but what I've done is start my own brand, the Jordan brand! Right now where working on a few color ways and samples but the fans are gonna love it!" As Nike watches on, an illusive feel-

ing of victory takes over her. Michael, though was favored by Nike decided to expand pass Nike, by taking a risk, something Droger encouraged.

Michael, became a God in his own right. His powers were stronger than that of Nike and Droger combine. The wager was complete. Droger had kept his word and was transformed into a mortal. As Michael returns home, he sees a man in the ball court. He walks over to get in a few shots, noticing it's Droger. A much older Droger playing a game, *Around the World.* Droger talks, "I wasn't mad at your choice son, not at all! You showed gusto and drive, and for that I favored you! It was the sacrifice of a God that allowed you to take a God's place. You have many people that look to your word now. Many people who will sacrifice their lifestyle for the blessing of yours. Many souls calling to you as they take a leap of faith. Remember what your doing it for! Cherish it!" Michael, holding his pose with the ball in his hand. He looks over, staring at Droger and responds. "Man, how much you got on this shot!?"

Aria was a victorious God, securing millions of new devoted believers. During their time up in the Northlands, Aria and her love, Piruphius, began to expand with new mortal leaders. Dryden calls to them to schedule a council meeting amongst Nero Gods. Dryden speaks of a war coming, a war amongst Gods, not just mortals. Dryden speaks of a prophecy given to him by the God Lufkin. Many of the Elbrus Gods were growing increasingly with rage at the thought that half of Aria new believers were those of Potis and Cephalos bloodline.

The Nero sound began to shine a light on trouble and depression that their people faced in the inner city as well as the Southland. Chaka Goddess of Funk and James, Godfather of Soul were two major Demi-Gods who pushed this cause. Because of their interest and pull to literature and language, they also praised Dryden. They were primary for bringing him freedom speakers, writers, and artists. Artist like Melvin Charles was appointed by Dryden to work close with Darious in creating a symbol for the Nero movement. The dagger he uses on the Nero flag, is Dryden's dagger. It was mainly used as a tool to open an enclosed letter or puncture an enemy. Piruphius stayed in the north land for sometime recruiting soldiers and warriors preparing for what might be one of the most defying wars in the American lands. Also, in the North is where Etoile thrived. She was able to find a sense of expression with garments and hairstyles, interchanging them throughout the seasons. She was the best-dressed amongst Gods and mortals and was legend to be disguised as a slave on a plantation to watch over her son. To her own vanity, she decided to wear the most daring and alluring pieces of clothing. This is what prompted, *Sundays Best,* during Cephalos religious ceremonies, bringing along the most presentable Nero.

Etoile loved when people who served her, approached her with a really nice outfit. Those who did not, she tend to not favor them. Shal-

low, quite more than most Gods, Etoile was also a great warrior Goddess, causally brandishing a small sharp blade from a swordfish beak.

During her time there, Etoile began to forge a romance with one God who govern those lands for some time. Mortals knew him as *Candyman,* but to her, his name was Daninus. An artist, and at time, was in love with another women he painted a portrait of decades ago. His body was lynched and covered in oil and honey and burned alive by follower of Elbrus deities. What saved his soul was a self-portrait he made prior to his death and blessings from Damu, a God who possessed the ability to give strength to the dead Nero. Etoile and Daninus complimented each other's taste, as they often showed up to events wearing the most exotic furs, linens and leathers. Etoile always looked forward to events or ceremonies simply for her display of clothing. After the Gods finished their duties for Dryden, most of them split into separate corners of the America landscape. Etoile decided to head east for her sister ceremony. This ceremony was held in the east where most of Aria older believers migrated towards during the early part of the 20th century. Aria and her lover, the God-King, Piruphius, arrived and were met with sons and daughters of her inspired offspring. It was in true Piruphius behavior to show support when the moment of celebration was not his, but someone he loves. Not a God of enormous public and private affection, but during the ceremony he decided to surprise Aria with a necklace.

Piruphius pulls out a case made of ebony wood. Inside, a bracelet with violin strings interwoven with his dog's whiskers for sturdiness. Plucked from his heartstrings, the last string, if played, calls on to Piruphius, for wherever he would be. Lufkin arrives greeting Aria. Bowing, he presents a silver fish as a trinket. Aria looks up to Piruphius and smiles. Lufkin steps back replying, "A new age is awaiting my Goddess!"

Sons and daughters of artist such as Otis Redding, Smokey Robinson, James brown, and Aretha Franklin came to support and praise of Aria. They presented gifts such as flutes, Ayele, Kundi harp and drums. Younger artists played instruments including electronic pianos, innovative snares, guitars with cooper string, performing songs their parents made. Some even brought forth, festive drinks along with hooch, wines and juices. As the children began to praise Aria, the ground began to rumble and crack. The sound was infectious, the Nero people of Congoian, Yoruba and Latin were all in suspense as they were unsure what was happening next. Aria in such serendipitous spirits, begins to absorb the gifts from her left ear. She then pours out a dark maroon liquid from her mouth and nipples. Modeling itself into a structural form, the liquid builds fingers, hands, arms and then a torso. Veins flow through a breast as their body reaches to the sky.

Henos, God of Modern Nero and Music, was the birth of what is known as Hip-Hop to mortals. He was attitude and charm. He stood there stout and majestic. There was a presence to him that was somewhat intimidating but alluring to mortals and Gods. His hair was short and sometimes would grow long enough for his God aunt to alternate into a braid. He lived amongst the rigged and expressive. In some worlds, Gods and man would consider Henos the most aggressive, while others will label him passionate. He grew mighty in a short time, developing more expounding thoughts daily. Henos voice was boastful. He often expressed the idea that music should be for healing and exclusive to the imagination of the Nero people. Often feeling anger at the idea that Cephalos and Potis offspring wanting to be around him. Henos, however, dabbled frequently with daughters of the Goddess Drogheda. What took many Gods centuries to accomplish, only took Henos months, as his believers and followers increased overnight. Distraught, his mother Aria, gradually formed an ill-will towards her own son in the years progressing. The message he carried was the same as hers,

but was more enticing to the new world and younger generation. After his first decade of breath in the North-East, he decided to head west with Taurean, a God he saw as a close ally. Henos also possessed the ability to affect a space without physically existing in it. His speech; slang became part of mortals conversational blueprint. Dressing and attire was also part of the language Henos birth. During a large festival where the Nero people celebrated their heritage of music and arts, Aria was seen on the grounds singing in a note similar to a note that is said to heal Piruphi-us, a vocal range between middle C and A. A Soprano, was one of the vocal expressions Aria shown and performed in front of the Gods. Sad-ly, many mortals that day, did not absorb Arias vocal range. This didn't discourage Aria. Her vocal height soared even louder and more glori-ous. She sounded all through the festival until a group of kids, walking toward the exit of the festival heard the harmonious tones ringing out.

A kid slows down and then pauses, blocking out the noise of the crowd and chaos, only hearing Aria's voice. It swept him off his feet, such a soothing rhythmic voice, he was captivated as he replies to himself, "Mm, music to my ears!" Arriving towards the end of her ballad, Aria opens her eyes and sees a young boy with a smile standing in front of her. With a gray shirt and ripped jeans and a bass guitar hanging off his back, Aria looks down at the boy and responds, "And what is your name young one!" Star struck, the young boy stands there trying to get a word out. "Sss, so, so, sorry, your voice! It's amazing!" The young boy looks off to see his friends walking ahead. "Mm, my friends, they left me! I have to catch up to them, but in my opinion mam! You were the best I've heard all day, no jive! I was ready to give up on this music thing until I heard you!" As he walks away smit-ten, he turns around and shouts to Aria, "Oh and sorry, my name is Rick!"

It was one of Potis most memorable attempts. To remove Nero men by sending them off to war to die in a slaughter with little to no aide from America's Gods. Most of the men survived off unity and the praise and favor from God Piruphius. Their call to him was mostly for peace and rest, as Lord Piruphius promised his believers their day of restitution will arrive soon. On their route back home, from war with Vietnam, the Nero soldiers found themselves hooked on the nipples of the Goddess, Josephine. She was looked to as a conduit for herbs and antidotes that were in constant use for soldiers to numb or stimulate them during the war.

Josephine was more of a spiritual and physical healer for Gods. Gods like Piruphius were healed using some of her potions and spells. Back home, the Nero Gods are called to a council meeting hosted by Lord Dryden. Dryden stands amongst them and speaks, "We are here today to speak on a dawn of the new man. Many of those who represent me have migrated out from the south. This will be our new ground zero, here up north.

I asked you all here today because I was given foresight by the help of Lufkin. The foresight of the Nero's destiny, a destiny to be a supreme race of the new American land. I see a vision of us forming such an alliance that our followers all move as one, through harmony, community, and league. My vision is simple, to achieve national dominance, our believers must build the idea of us in their minds. Creating monuments, and paintings and mosaics of us erected throughout America's highlands.

We are and have been duplicated in many forms for years now. What we need is a symbol. Many of our followers have never seen us in true form. We need them to see something tangible! We will be impenetrable whereas, no army, nor race, nor government can overlook our message and culture." Aria responds, "You want a mega treaty!?" Dryden confirms with

a nod. "Yes, an alliance that forms all of the first-generation Nero Gods. Since Eve, no God possesses the strength as a Supreme." Looking at Piruphius, Dryden walks towards him placing his hand on his shoulder, "Your Mightiness! The Fire starter! With your victories and strategic unitizing, you are essential to this mega treaty, Lord Piruphius! The breath of my words and brass from your sword shall reward us of our goal through the journey of opportunity and challenge of obstacle." Dryden continues, I am here to also offer in return to each God, followers of mine that will be followers of yours. Making you stronger and greater than you've ever been."

I ask for your army and in return, I will grant a place for your soldiers to rest. I understand my brother you seek to contain peace of mind! There is a place out west you will find gratifying!" Along were Goddess, Imani and Orizah. Imani was the driving force of hope, faith, and love. She was the right brain of the mega treaty. Orizah, was essential in providing the nourishment side of the meeting. "Without this, we are divided and misguided like many mortals, blindly following the latest trend or belief into a path of never ending hunger. We cannot afford to lead our followers to a place of neglect. The followers that look to me for literary guidance will not last. Many of my followers are being hung, killed and captured by speaking the words I translate. This alliance will ensure that we are all protected."

Dryden begins to move storms and clouds, showing the Gods a glimpse into his chosen. "I've been watching him for some time, he has potential and will be the pioneer as a new Nero leader." Piruphius along with Aria and Imani observe the mortal, in agreement, "He seems pretty green, Dryden." Dryden tries to soothe their concern, "Ah yes, we've all shown moments of naivety, but he's ready, he's been chosen. I've witnessed his involvement within his community. Young, yet he has shown strength in speak-

ing up against those who denounce his culture and background. A convinced Piruphius approaches Dryden. "As promised brother…" Piruphius impressed with himself, provides four thousand men, ready to move at the command of Dryden word. Months progress as the chosen leader Huey formed an elite organization throughout his neighborhood. Along with his fellow activist and speakers, they branched out to start new chapters in different cities and states. As they took their pilgrimage to the north, the Nero Gods were there waiting. Many of the Gods stumbled into the Goddess Etoile. She was a Goddess of Glamour and Confidence. Dryden questioned if and how she arrived there before the rest of the deities.

Composed Etoile responds, "Dryden, What I do here is not your, nor anyone else matter of worry." Dryden speculated based on Etoile's promiscuous ways, she was secretly seeing the one they called, *Candyman*. He ruled the Northlands as a dark spirit, half God-half Ghost. A legend of calling his name several times would bring about his reign to the land. This legend was rumored by a Elbrus mortal who visited some time ago. Etoile played with this idea of calling his name often testing him during their intimate encounters. He also was an artist of sorts, painter mostly. He went around painting mostly God portraits. Daninus, or Candyman lost his painters hand to Potis after he discovered a portrait of Drogheda in the nude.

Many other spirits were called on while there in the North. The Goddess Orizah offered a blessing, which allowed Dryden's chosen, Huey and the Panthers to host a children breakfast program which served over ten thousand youth. Their movement, so large in media coverage, caused a peaked interest and concern for one of Potis offspring and head generals, Magnus. A God of Destruction and Chaotic order, in control of laws and the mortals in authority of them. Magnus possessed the ability to see anyone and anything as a threat along with a greater ability to destroy that threat. With this

level of power, many suggested he held more status than his father Potis. Reaching out to Potis, Magnus suggested that the Panthers were using Orizah's food to coax Potis impressionable youth, inevitably turning his people against him. Potis talking aloud to his son, "I'm aware of how these animals can regroup and assemble, it is necessary to intervene now. We must always protect what is ours and if not, before we know it, Drogheda offspring will bear their children."

"I can handle this!" Magnus appointing himself eagerly. Head high, Potis has an epiphany. "No! I have someone in mind, a being that can go in-depth and can give me more insight better than any man or God can." Potis sent for one of his followers. A high school coach in the Westlands who brought the mighty Goddess, Nike to America. Potis knew with her by his side, he will reign supreme. Bill, Nike's liaison, is told to arrange a meeting where Potis wanted to meet the Goddess. Nike, somewhat impressed by Potis, sees him as an analogous to the mighty Zeus. Hearing his proposition, Nike knew that with Bill rebranding Nike in America and Potis granting access to his elites, she will be ruler yet again.

Potis expresses, "The followers I grant you are the most devoted. They will pass down generations of wealth. They have enough buying-power to hold you into existence for centuries to come. They have been blessed by my brother Cephalos with the ability to be overlooked as a threat. Their ability to camouflage their true intentions has granted them access to become Lords and Kings that rule these lands in secret." As Nike is pleased to hear this, she goes out to seek more information of the Nero Gods and their believers' habits and behaviors. Within only a several days, Nike returns with a strategy. With certainty, she shares, "There are a few tactics I see that can cripple the organization. This strategy, if done carefully will dismantle them in a matter of ten years." Potis in a joyous mood,

"You are more cunning than that of my brother Cephalos. What is the first step?" What Nike proposed was several stages of infiltration. A crucial first step was starting with his lover and kin, Goddess Drogheda's daughter to slay a God named Tyrothion. They were Nymphs that have been controlled and restrained under Potis enchantment. Drogheda, the High Goddess of all Nymphs in the new land, was able to mobilize them to do the dirty work. Drogheda Nymphs reported back to her over the course of the next few months, observing Huey and his organization. After many years of longing for such lifestyle, accompanied with lack of resources and addictions, the Tribesman were no match for such seductive illusions. These women were called, Hybrids of the Nymphs, non-black, nor white, but featured alluring traits from both races of woman. They possessed a unique ability to extract information and strategies even from the immortals themselves.

Though Huey was easy to access publicly, one Hybrid decided to infiltrate members of the party upward, crippling them entirely. Starting with a police officer whom secretly worked for Huey, was seduced by a Goddess and daughter of Drogheda, Aunjanue. She knew when to let a man speak his way into his own grave, and sometimes provided the shovel. A man's ego was her playground and manipulating this officer was like riding a seesaw. Aunjanue played with John's mind and heart. She began to pit him against Huey, not just being a better lover, but a better man all around. This fueled John into a jealous rage, leading him to seek Huey and abuse his authority. Pursuing Huey and his associates, Officer John was able to spot Huey, by identifying his car Huey was in the back seat of. Catching up to the car to try to arrest Huey, Huey's associates scuffle with John, turning the situation into a shootout. The favor of Dryden and Piruphius led Huey to safety, but death of Officer John. After these altercations, Huey felt a sense of God-like immunity. His actions became more reckless by betraying a Godly code, harming

one of Drogheda's followers who was a sex worker. The chosen one fell into deep waters. Once he began to lose his purpose and guidance, he also began to lose his voice, resulting in Huey relying on using mortal weapons against his "enemies." Huey's actions gave Magnus leverage to bring forth his arrest, placing Huey in captivity. Dryden believed this to be a perfect time to speak with Huey directly. Huey seemed to suffer intense withdrawals and delusion. Mumbling to himself sitting on the caged cell floor. Dryden approaches as a small black cat.

First, he purrs rubbing against the bars and then speaks, "I see a deep frustration in you. I see the inevitably of self-destruction. I'm still processing if this is an act of environment or genetic. I need you to understand many speakers before you have made this error which cost them their lives and lives of many around them. You were given access to worldly things and used them in excess. You are responsible for your own consumption young master." Huey relapsing and incoherent, snaps out of it, "What do you mean!? I'm not sure if what you see is self-destruction! As a God it was your responsibility to make sure these vices did not affect me! You made me a vessel of your word. You gave me a life without preparation for it. You placed me in the center of these things knowing I was not ready." The black cat continues, "I placed you there and gave you resources. You developed, and along with your growth your ego matured." Huey in anger replies, "Ego!" Dryden replies, "Yes ego! It is a mortal's ego to assume you do not need the tools to restrain from temptation. How dare you fall short of my capabilities, I am Lord Dryden, I am your vessel for bridging the threads between generations, no Nero mortal can do this without me" Huey looks down to the floor shaking his head with a smirk, "Ha- a mortal ego! Right!?" A rambling Huey continued his tirade while captive. Dryden often returned to him in many forms, such as a prison guard, a lawyer, and even a butterfly. Huey was distraught and did not want to associate himself with any of the

Nero Gods that had given him previous favor. Huey fell into deep despair. Huey replies, "I suffered too long belonging solely to one religion or group that no longer serves me and to exit this place of captivity, Magnus has offered me a pardon if I am to denounce the league and deities associated." In spitefulness, Dryden places Huey under a spell, leaving his words lost on his own people. Unfortunately, this spell also has a mirror affect on the enchanter, leaving Dryden's gospel somewhat mute to his followers as well.

These cause and effects would leave room for other leaders under Dryden to be a vulnerable target to likes of Potis and Magnus. Most of the leaders seen Huey as the final hope for making a true change. Potis saw this as a time to strike, seeing how only secondary leaders were now in command, mismanaging the remaining Nero soldiers on the front line. It was only a matter a time before the domino effect took place. Many of the soldiers needed protection in preparation for a potential war. Piruphius army would go seek Darious. Darious was a God of Fabrication and Craft. He was known for salvaging leather amour and premium clothing from many other Gods or Demi-Gods after their reign. Darious was also great at making advanced equipment for Piruphius such as his helmet made of pangolin skin. This amour Darious often forged would protect Nero from temporary conflicts interacting with man-made weapons and along with spiritual elements such as attacks on self-esteem, confidence and self-worth. Magnus sent many of his pigment police into the Panthers territory. Many of the Panthers men were killed or injured. Potis arrived into the land to play a part in the destruction. Potis swollen with violence, escalates the matter by raping and killing some of the women and men in battle. Such involvement directly with humans was forbidden as Nike witnessing this felt a bit off-put. Buildings blown to pieces as most of the Gods came to save their surviving followers. Most of Piruphius believer's that survived, were captive or ran into exile.

Like lost sheep, they prayed for help from their Lord. The anger the soldiers harbored, created an wedge with Piruphius and a disconnect with Dryden speakers. Piruphius called on his hound, Jaubauis, a Doberman, to search for Potis amongst the terrain. There was no sight of him nor Magnus and their men. Overhearing sound of tears, he notices a woman hurt laying amongst the wreckage. The closer he arrived to the cry, he sees Aunjanue lying there. Looking in close distance, he sees Drogheda approaching. Drawing his weapon as she approaches, he demands to see Potis. Distraught Drogheda steps back responding, "This is too much! He has gone too far. All these bodies that have lived, and laughed. I want him gone as much as you."

Potis quickly appears, lunging a small car. Drogheda, pushing Piruphius out of the way, swinging her shield from her hip deflecting the car. She charges toward him as Potis jumps over her, landing on top of her with his foot to her face planted into gravel. He grabs the dagger from her ankle, "You disloyal whore!" As Potis begins to strike, Potis is struck in the jaw by Piruphius, stumbling back off Drogheda, dropping the blade. Potis calls on his son Magnus and his men to regroup. Gods and Demi-Gods and soldiers all begin to battle once more.

Piruphius threw extreme blows, striking and killing some of Potis men. Potis hurls a sharp spear into the crowd of Nero soldiers. Damu, Piruphius brother, joins in to fight off most of Potis offspring. Dryden then casts dark clouds of black ink in the sky to deflect Potis and the other Gods. This cloudiness was a weapon Dryden would use to create confusion. Dryden's son Taurean, in the dark mist took advantage to attack men underneath Magnus. Taurean never carried a weapon. His fists were dangerous and his hit was deadly. One direct hit from Taurean could kill a Bull instantly. Potis struggling to get away, reaches his hand out to Magnus to help. Magnus pulling him up from the brawl

comments, "I've witnessed their resilience! Nike was wrong father! We need to regroup and strike another day! You've tortured and raped their woman and destroyed their pride, yet they seem stronger than ever!"

As Potis is helped up, he calls Drogheda to come home. With no response from her, he noticed Piruphius picking her up from the ground. He steps back to notice Dryden and the other Gods are there to protect Drogheda. He leaves with a forewarning to the Nero's, "Whether now or later, you shall remember your place!" Suddenly, Dryden is pushed in the chest by Piruphius while letting out a Godly shout, "And where were you!? Your leaders neglected my men, some of them are now held captive. I was able to rescue some Dryden, but my believers are dying. You swore to me!" Dryden gathers himself, "I should have known, it was my own desperation. I favored him to be the pioneer, the voice, the future. I now understand." As Dryden continues, "Huey and many others at this time have yet to witness it, for they were the first wave of soldiers to push through the political barricade. I see for the mortals, what stands on the other side of that barricade is not freedom at all, but vices; more hurdles, capital, sex, celebrity, and lore."

Piruphius calms his temper. "Lord Dryden, as I began watching your apostles in your absence, I, too, now understand what they yearn for. A form of means. Means that can changed their lives and the families of which they are far from. To a mortal, it is everything, it is the key to freedom. To us Gods, it is an illusion. I see now that this freedom they seek is an enchantment placed by Cephalos on the Nero. A mist, to give the Nero Creator, the Motivator and the Slave, an imaginary win."

Piruphius finds a safe place for the woman he found crying. "Aunjanue, she's pregnant with a child from one of my soldiers. Her child will be one of ours now. She needs healing and rest." As the Nero Gods bring their dead

back to the afterlife, Dryden suggests to Orizah to watch over Aunjanue. Drogheda was wounded as well, but could not be treated by Orizah, being a Goddess of Elbrus spirit. Therefore, Nike returns to her aide. Drogheda sends for Dryden and Piruphius to meet with her after their encounter.

A healing Drogheda sits and speaks, "You trusted your followers too strongly and I too made this mistake. My followers have grown from the days of mere sexual exploitation. They are maturing. Soon will the days past where my believers souls are puppets from the strings of Potis and Magnus. They fear his absence and lack of interest more than they fear their own lack of self-worship and individuality. They shall have their freedom. The dominant woman is the future. A woman of own mind and body and freewill. No more shall my believers be trapped, I see a future of the optimized woman, able to do as she please with power, confidence and control. Is this not what you want for your people!? I hear you cry out for the future of the Nero American. To do so requires a sacrifice, a loss of not just one, but many. I've lived for centuries on this land, and lands before this one to see what it takes. Your people have not years, but centuries to go."

Dryden absorbs the message. Dryden ask, "I debate what your suggesting is that we have done something wrong?" In response, Drogheda replies, "Wrong in the sense of calculating distance, not direction. You see, I saw your mission, but it only involved that of the Nero race. I believe we can fight this war together. To even pass through the portals of Drahmen, your people will need my help. We have shared trauma from the likes of Potis." The unsold Dryden replies, "Yes, but you've benefited off the trauma of my people's addictions, temptations, and sexual interest for years." Piruphius interjects, "I think this can work Dryden, we have not tried this. Let's expand our message! Some of Drogheda's souls are that of Nero blood as well. I know your frustration, but she's right. Most of the challenges the

Neros face are that of Lord Drahmen, from not having the ability or resources to adapt from obstacle to opportunity. We should try this Dryden!" Dryden decides to agree with this expansion. In turn, he decides to take several Gods with him to the Eastlands to spread the message. The first God was Imani, the Goddess of Hope, Triumph, Resilience and Belief. The second God was Orizah, the Goddess of Nourishment and Healing. The third Goddess was Aria, the spirit in which brought forth healing in song and tale. Lastly was his son, Taurean, God of (New) Language and Aura. Piruphius decides to head west along with his brother Damu. Drogheda follows, which leads to the inception of the second civil and feminist movement.

As years progressed, Drogheda's people were placed in the forefront of the movement, pushing Nero's message towards the tail end of global concern. In a conflict with Drogheda, Piruphius leaves the land to be with his wife Aria. Aria and Piruphius spent some time on the east momentarily. Though they had several children, she was soon ready to birth now another. During a ceremony in worship of Aria, she was showered with gifts from the sons and daughters of many musicians, fashionistas and cultural attaché' of the community. Some followers gift handcrafted instruments such as a drums, horns, and shells with harmonic strings. Gods were in attendance, including God of Guidance, Lufkin. He brought along a crabs claw for safe access across the sea and a fish as a blessing. Piruphius had a gown made for Aria by Darious, embellished with stones from Sierra Leone along with a custom instrument made of heartstrings. Though Dryden was still in bad ways with Piruphius after the movement with Drogheda, Dryden still offers Aria an array of furniture, books, and vases. However, Piruphius took a liking to his son Taurean, offering him an opportunity to visit his land. As loved ones celebrate, Lufkin looks to Dryden stating that a prophet is coming. "A son of Gods and a son of man! I foresee they will be the connection to unify

and excel all. Isn't this your wish!? It is coming Dryden!" Dryden replied, "My excitement is lost on the idea my good friend. I've spent countless decades in attempt to achieve that goal, but I fear it will be something even us Gods may not be around to witness." The roars of Arias followers increase, as she suddenly brings forth the birth of Piruphius and her son, Henos. The God Henos was born. Henos, like Dryden, possessed the ability to join generations together. For Henos, he was able to bridge several generations, not just one or two. In addition, he can manipulate sound, art and rhythms. His presence shifted environments, whether in physical form or spiritual. Young offspring from Elbrus Gods, took a liking to Henos, making Potis and his brothers more vindictive. His mother, Aria, suffered from a conflicting emotion of envy of her son's rapid praise. In the spirit of being divine, she decided to head to the Westlands.

Aria and Piruphius had multiple offspring in their journey back west. One of many sons was the Mighty Tyrothion, a brother of Henos. A great ruler and God of Rebellion and Expression. He would be the symbol for Tribes music and culture in the west. He and his father often disagreed. Piruphius believed this was due to his son bringing outsiders into what he would call his *Tribe*. The Tribes were broken up into small groups called Leagues, Chapters, or Sets. Some of these Sets were made up of over two to three hundred men. To join most of Piruphius Tribes, it required several steps of action. One action was the ability to fight and defend. Another was the bloodline connection within your Tribe. The more members that were related, the stronger the Tribe. Tyrothion men were more experienced in fights likely with the use of weapons. Most of Piruphius original Tribesmen were genetically stronger and much more brute, yet, also wise and strategic and calculated in attacks and ideas. Building out in the west, Piruphius leaders Trion and Koden were

amongst the strongest. They were essential in the concept to protect and serve their communities. This is what Piruphius wanted. As general of generals, Taurean would be in charge of accepting or denying new recruits in the Tribe within communities. Taurean found himself to be a great warrior, an O.G. he often called him. Taurean brought a sense of style and swag when he entered a space. He was innovative, he was one of the first Gods to mark himself with tattoos and wear man-made jewelry. He showed a sense of respect for both man and God. He was a bull in stature, so Piruphius soldiers embraced him as one of their own. This chain of command made Tyrothion quite annoyed with his father decisions. When his father would be gone most of the time, it was Tyrothion, who kept his original soldiers in the Tribes favored. Tyrothion believed Taurean was favored because of his physical appearance, as Tyrothion saw himself as plump. In later arguments, Piruphius confessed that his men respect Taurean, but feared his own son.

Tyrothion oversaw many of the initiations into the Tribes. Some of the initiations constituted a ritual such as dance, fight, and challenging obstacles. In most cases it was a fight between a soldier against civilian or potential member. Tyrothion was known for being somewhat a bully towards civilians and otherwise, inserting himself in some of the fights to cause more of a disadvantage to the newcomer. He would sometimes say "…life isn't easy, so why should we make it easy." He had several brothers, some much older, but he was considered to be the oldest based on his outspoken-take-charge demeanor. The fear the soldiers had for Tyrothion created a division between groups, becoming turbulent. There was a rumor for years that a man can become a God themselves from the blood of a God. Many attempted, but the rumor was never authenticated. Oaken, wanted to retest this theory. He was a new and eager member trying to prove his point as a worthy believer to Tyrothion. As everyone

spectates the initiation, Oaken gets closer to the front of the crowd. Without hesitation, he pulls out his weapon to fire a shot. Taurean, with quick movement, avoids the shot, as it instantly kills Taurean's soldier! Everyone stood back in great shock, taking a minute to register what took place. Oaken, drops the weapon and flees. Days follow, as Taurean and his men were on the hunt for him. Taurean eventually approached Tyrothion asking for him to bring forth the man responsible to face righteous punishment. Tyrothion, already dismissive of the idea of Taurean, pushes him away, causing Taurean to grab his wrist then punching Tyrothion in the face. Piruphius felt torn. Though he had several reasons to disagree with his son, he could not go against him. Piruphius tells Taurean that all leaders can meet in a neutral territory to try to come to a peaceful resolution. Gods and Demi-Gods alike, met to discuss the future of their treaty. Instead they met in what was known as, Battle of the Leagues. Wrestling and grappling ensued as men were ripped about by Gods. Piruphius, charges into the center of both Gods bout, splitting the Tribes in half for centuries. Taurean decided to detach his Tribe members from Piruphius and Tyrothion altogether.

As their tension increased, Tyrothion, in better spirits with his father, suggested bringing Dryden or his son, Taurean into the light, by targeting one of their favored. Piruphius wasn't actually keen to this way of colliding with Gods. There was an immortal law, Gods are punished for the killing of mortal men. Impatient of his father's indecisiveness, Tyrothion instigates an idea that Piruphius is growing weak. In anger, Piruphius plucks Tyrothion off his feet from his neck. "You infant! Don't ever question my command! As a God, you must predict your own results of an action you caused! If we as Gods, begin to break our own rules, then what is a God!" Tyrothion embarrassed and afraid of looking weak to his Tribe members, secretly sends for Oaken to kill Huey. Huey, released from Magnus after some years, was rumored to be involved with what the ancestral Nero's Gods call, "Bi". A sin in the

eyes of the Gods, where one promotes self-destruction for mortal profits. Walking out of an alley, Huey encounters now Captain, Oaken. Standing there, Huey looks at him, growing agitated knowing who has sent him. Huey yells, "I don't give a fuck about them or give a fuck about you! What the hell you gonna do!?" Oaken, hesitates for a moment before feeling a sense of obligation to a cause. After a quick thought, Huey lays bleeding to death from gunshots. As Tribes grew distant, Piruphius primary leaders took notice to the financial gain from the same path Huey chose. Tribes began to see more money than Gods themselves. Ironically, they couldn't sell or market these drugs outside of their own neighborhood, an imprisoned spell cast by God, Magnus. A spell learned from his Uncle Cephalos. Other troubles that followed with drugs, arrived from God, Weogufka. *Hooch,* a drink mixed with mineral oil, hydrocarbons and grains was a mind alternating compound created on accident by Weogufka. Potis decided to implement the potion into the new land towards the end of the Civil Rights War on Piruphius men. Leaving them confused, addicted and stifled. This curse was deadly to mortals and immortals alike. Gods never truly dabbled with man-made compounds and agents. The affects and lingering marks it would leave on man, would be much more disastrous to Demi or full Gods. Humans who fell under the spell of this potion would be held in an everlasting charm.

They were called, junkies and alcoholics. For Gods, their remedies came from enchantress and Goddess, Josephine. She was primarily a healer, mainly for Gods and Demi-Gods that contain immortal wounds. Humans were introduced to her when her son, Weogufka, decided to steal her potions and chemicals to make his own liquid substances for celebrations and rituals. Weogufka often gave mortals who attended, micro-doses of these chemicals. Piruphius fell into a Godly despair, seeing his Tribesman in the land of Piru, facing crippling addictions and profiting off their own people addictions.

The God Henos arrived to the Westland during this era. His presence and aura influenced a large number of the believers there. His time there was often to see one of his many true lovers, Afeni. She was an Icon of humans and favored by Dryden. She helped organize and conduct rallies back east. She was in a romantic relationship with Henos during her stay in the East. Together, out of five offspring, they birthed the Demi-God, Lesane. Highly favored by the great Dryden and Godson to Taurean, he was protected spiritually. Henos and Taurean began to have a long-standing relationship due to similar interest. One interest was woman, the other was their dislike for Piruphius Tribe members. Lesane showed great leadership and self-worth. He started writing poetry as a youth, from listening to his mother write to Dryden. Henos wasn't necessarily a bad father to his children, but a neglectful one. Most times torn between his obligations to many of his followers, friends and lovers. Many men after Henos came to the aid of Afeni and her young but fell short of being attentive to her children's needs. Lesane gained recognition through connections of his mother and Henos' blessings. Henos provided him with tools and musical agents to aide Lesane passion. Outspoken and charismatic, Lesane was given an opportunity to join a musical band, performing throughout vast arenas and venues. In Lesane's works of writing, he would declare his lust and admiration for woman. Lesane began to have a lustful romance with Demi-Goddess, Madonna. This courtship was forbidden for centuries even amongst Gods. As a Demi-Goddess, Madonna still had to answer to Drogheda. Many of her predecessors despised her, she was one of the deviant and rebellious Demi-Goddesses.

Lesane grew favorable to his grand Godfather Piruphius. This favor granted him access into Tribes home. His music and aura created a unity around the Tribes. Piggybacking off of Lesane favor and blessing, some members from Tribes were able to achieve their pas-

sions and desires, as musicians or as Icons. His form of art also brought Taurean's Tribes to the same spaces. Taurean often brought gifts to these functions, mostly cannabis from Weogufka. Weogufka provided multiple concoctions of hooch and moonshine for southern folk since before Abraham release of the Nero. Leaders of the Tribes would come together to perform a ritual. A dance of celebration of Tribes united. Shortly into the celebrations, word spread that Dryden arrived. Lesane, standing in between both Gods, demanded a friendly truce.

Dryden extends his hand offering Piruphius a basket of grapes, a gold balaclava made of pangolin and feathers from Potis bird Aeoris, as a peaceful gesture. Piruphius embraces him with a wink and smile as they hug. "As a brother, our differences should not distant us, but bring us closer. And for that I am sorry." Tyrothion, watching, grows annoyed of his father's friendship with Dryden and walks away to socialize throughout the event. Tyrothion informed his nephew Lesane of his careless acts and his inflated ego. Combining and alternating his alliance with selected Tribes will have ramifications and can cost him his life. Lesane refused to heed Tyrothion message, seeing this as a sign of jealously. Lesane became one of the few Demi-Gods to address his status publicly to the world. In a romance with Lesane, Madonna wanted to introduce him to one of the Supreme Gods, Medusa. In doing so, Lesane was blindly fascinated with Medusa, forming an attachment he could not break. Lesane wanted Medusa to make an appearance with him almost anywhere he went. Though Medusa was of Nero blood, she was not fond of the Nero American people, but was still able to absorb the idea of his praise and worship to her. To praise her, with or without her physical presence, a necklace and clothing was made of her face from Gianni, was gifted to Lesane. This infatuation brought her many followers and believers of the Nero people. After returning west, leaving an event, Taurean, without warning attacks

a man. As everyone joins the scuffle, Lesane jumps in to defend Taurean. Lesane showed the strength of Henos and his Grandfather Piruphius, leaving the man almost unconscious. Fleeing the situation, Lesane ask, "Who was that!?" Taurean replies, "Some guy name Oaken!" Now at a traffic light, Lesane sees a car window rolling down next to him. A man shouts to him, "Hey!" Lesane quickly looks over to see gunshots blaring. Gods and mortals from all over attended the funeral of Lesane. Piruphius, the God of Assembly and Community, spoke. "This was an issue of Gods close involvement with managing mortals insecurities. We've all had a hand in trying to fix or help their situations. I say from this moment on, we shall assist from a place of protection, a boundary with man entirely. We've involved ourselves enough and we've lost. We lost allies, land, and now, Gods!" As Henos mourns, he does not offer any words at his sons funeral. He simply kisses Afeni and fly's off, leaving the American lands.

Jerry was a coworker for a local floral & lumber shop. He carried himself with flamboyance when feeling confident. Jerry, after work, took the longer way back home. In a family of five brothers, three sisters, Jerry, as the middle child was picked on from siblings daily. Jerry older brother would poke him with a broom stick until he would ball up in a corner, "Youa real sissy boy huh!? Get up sissy! Straight bitch! Quit ya cryin'!" His younger brothers and sisters questioned Jerry's masculinity when he couldn't do something as simple as kill a fly that crept into their mother's window screen.

His father, Jerry Senior, always had words for his spooked son, "I raised you to be a man. It's who you are, it's you standing up for yourself son!" Something Jerry heard often as his father placed ice and bandages on him. An exhausted Jerry Jr., "But there are friends I have who I don't have to fight! Don't have to second guess their actions or words. We can communicate!"

His father calmly, "Son... No matter who you stand with, you always have to fight for something you believe in. My thought- ...well question rather, to you is this, why not fight for a belief with your people!? I see you out there with your friends making plans- Make plans with your real family! Ya hear me!" Jerry looked up at his father wanting to say more, but there wasn't going to be any empathy that night.

At work, Jerry developed a rapport with a few coworkers who shared Jerry's troubles. "You know if we want!" A coworker conjures an idea, "We can follow him, the one they call, *Flowerboy*. Yea, ha-ha, you guys laugh-but I'm telling you..." Jerry took very little convincing, showing up with other nomads to wait in the vast crop lands of central America. As they prayed for Flowerboy's return, many came with a trade. Some with a call to the winds, offering of clothes; stripping themselves down to nude, as well as spelling symbols and signs in the crops. To mortals, what they see is simply a rainbow. This rainbow was Juniper's ladder in escaping the immortal realm. Through hail and storm,

Juniper would come down wearing an androgynous hair style and shells and pearls as necklace. Though his believers prayed to him through the sacrifice of their garments, he himself barely wore anything. Juniper was the son of the Supremacy God, Potis. Potis and Juniper argued a lot and caused Juniper to travel to mortal land often finding enjoyment elsewhere. Juniper, God of Exploration and Sexual Journey, was full of chatter and social networking. He got along mostly with Goddess of the Nero race and culture. Juniper could only be seen in a lighting seconds and then would swish off into the distance. Jerry caught a whiff of Junipers stardust, which gave him the temporary ability of direction from a God.

Juniper's believers were seen as indifferent from the rest of their peers. They showed a heighten interest in lustful desires towards all species. An impulsive Jerry, dropped the flowers he brought for Juniper and ran screaming in excitement with the rest of his friends through the crops. They headed to the Eastland finding a place where many of those who were unique like Jerry could build a community. In several months, Jerry developed friendships with socialites and artist in the community. They filled their days with coffee and window shopping and their nightlife with incognito party events.

Dancing along with his friends, Jerry is shouted to in his ear about beings named Potis and Magnus. They were father and sibling to Juniper and their believers frequently sought vengeance on Junipers followers. It was said that Juniper's brother, Magnus, had men sent to raid their event. The music was cut abruptly, as police shout and knock down men and women. Bottles and trays were thrown at patrons from the police, leaving them bleeding and screaming trying to exit through a narrow basement steps.

A few days later Jerry meets up with his friends in a bar as they conduct a strategy to stand against Magnus and his men. Jerry shouts, "I'm all for it! I'm here and I've been tired for too long! I have been bullied, judged and isolated way too long. Here! Now! I find a place where I belong and feel at

home. So much has been taken from me and this will not be taken from me!" Jerry & friends plan went into effect that night, as most of Juniper's followers were anticipating a potential raid at a local spot titled, Stonewall. Having the best time of his life, Jerry hears a woman getting grabbed up by police near the exit. Kicking and screaming, the women begins shouting, "Why don't ya fucking do something!?" As associates gathered around, cocktails were thrown and gunshots blasted. Juniper and Magnus men went to war. Some of Juniper's men were castrated and brutally beaten half to death. A few of Magnus men were hurt but suffered little damage due to having armor.

Jerry and his comrades went a grueling six days of war prevailing against Magnus and his men. This stance, gained Juniper's followers a national victory, even developing a symbol of his presence in the form of the rainbow. As tides settle between Juniper and his brother, Jerry and his friends returned back to a small café shop a bit later. Bruised and cut up, they joke about how some of the police enjoyed the grappling of some of Juniper's men.

The café door then opens as a group of men walk in laughing. Jerry quickly looks in the other direction to avoid eye contact. One of Jerry's friends, still talking amongst themselves, spot Jerry's energy of discomfort. "Yea I know how you feel Jerry, they don't understand us!" As they all begin to agree, one of the men laugh, "Yea, if only they fought the way we did, they would get what they want!" Jerry questions his friend, "Bruce, whatcha mean dear!? They?" He replies, "Come on Jerry! They've been a problem to us for a while now. Them Niggers! Every time I see them, I get the same chill you do. Come on Curtis, you even said it the other day! Don't look at me like I'm the only one who feels it. I just hate Niggers!"

Most musicians after Robert, grew from his songs, inspired and righteous. Many Nero people looked for ways to publicly display their talents after what Robert accomplished. In desperation, some musicians and even some God musicians looked to Oculus, brother to Cephalos, God of Foresight and Exploitation. Some of the Nero talents made deals with Oculus over Aria due to the assumption of a safe passage through the space in which, Drahmen, God of Obstacle and Opportunity, rest. These deals usually lead to Nero men and woman also praising Cephalos' six sons.

Cephalos was the High God in charge of slaves coming to America. He oversaw the structure of his sons running the plantations and land to keep in order. Many Nero such like Robert, remained on a lower tier plantation. These plantations all around America were based on a number system; One, being lower and hundred being the highest. The lowest tier slaves were treated harshly and barely ate or bathed. The higher tier slaves were treated more *fairly*, having access to more clothes, rags, shoes, meals. However, no tier allowed the reading and writing of slaves and community of slaves. When currency was being printed, Cephalos, went to his nephew, Magnus to favor an artist to immortalize his sons on these bills. Walter Disney was an artist who worked closely with Magnus. He was no mortal nor immortal, but an Icon. Benjamin Franklin was one of Cephalos' favorite. He ruled over thousands of slaves and held status amongst political and social clubs. This granted his son Benjamin to become embellished on the hundred dollar bill.

Oculus and his brother, Cephalos, were in the business of control. One God in control of body the other God in control of soul. Oculus benefited from the desperation of the Nero artist with Faustian deals more deadly than the one offered by Papa Legba to Robert. Most of the artist souls were held captive by the God Oculus even after death, paying a debt Oculus felt was owed. Oculus believers often followed Potis in his principals of entitlement and

privilege. One in particular, was a little boy inspired by Nero music. He was favored by the Gods for his dedication of mimicking and fabricating doppelgangers of these Nero musicians. Many of his carbon copies resembles the likes of Arias followers such as Muddy Waters and Chuck Barry. Oculus, sfavored the little boy, Sam, as a protégé. His claim to this favor was once Sam found and groomed an artist by the name of Elvis.

Some artist fled the states in search of more acceptance and opportunities elsewhere. Many of the earlier followers were able to meet with Aria and her servants for counsel. Gathering around Aria, she replies amongst a hasty crowd, "It is alright children, no mortal, no God shall tarnish your legacy as musicians. I swore to Robert that no harm will come to them unless afflicted upon. Their dance will end shortly and they will be forced out."

One of the musicians enslaved to Oculus deal, steps up and replies, "My Glory, you understand they have this white-ass country-boy stealing our songs, we're losing money, status and credibility and our fans- ya dig!" Aria looks on in anger. "Being a Nero requires more work. This is true. You must produce a new style a new groove. Are you afraid to adapt? We Gods strategize decades- not days. I've seen this Elvis and Sam duo, studying, taking notes of my believers and trying to learn your ways. I say what is true when I say, it was *I* who gave voice and song to this land! I sprung the roots from their seed and caressed the winds swiftly through the mountains, shacks, and alleys! You are my blood and soul! You all will prevail, it is in your nature.! And with favor amongst the High Gods, these times create more inspiration and drive. I shall cast my enchantments over those who wish to excel. A dawn of the exceptional talented Nero people will arrive." As Aria spoke, so did her actions. A mortal named Barry, was favored by Cephalos. Barry's father, Berne, was a slave owner and bloodline to Cephalos. Barry's mother, was a Nero slave, whose blessings was from

Aria, as his mother would sing to her in the field and the night for healing. With Barry having interracial parents, it allowed the young Barry to travel through obstacles with very little interruptions from Drahmen.

Meeting with Cephalos, Oculus, and Dryden, Aria knew a deal would have to be made to excel her people. In their treaty, she suggests the God's offspring, Bernie, relinquish the slaves that possess the gift of speech and harmony. Stern and forceful, "You have enough of my people held captive, what is one less plantation!?" She knew what they wanted, they wanted the source, they wanted Robert Johnson. A trade not worth it in her heart. She calls out a list of athletes and musicians that towed the line of Nero and Elbrus belief. She replied, "You can have *them*!" Souls that showed slightly more interest in Oculus. Aria hands off these souls to Cephalos and Oculus as Dryden aids the treaty as a mediator. Somewhat pleased, Cephalos replies, "That will do just fine!"

In an act to oblige the treaty, what mortals witnessed was the release of Lefkos clan. A gang under Potis that were sent to catch- better yet, chase out most of the Nero's from the southland. For this plan to work, Berne was to be considered a, "Niggerlover," one of the worst forms of betrayal to mortals who praise Potis. A small whisper to the winds, Aria moved an entire family from the Southlands up to the North.

During young Barry's stay in the north, he found an alliance with a man name Jackie. This friendship began to grow, as Aria knew Barry would be favored through the realm of *Fugue*. All mortals, knowing or unknowingly cross this realm. It is where one is met by Lord Drahmen. He is essentially a gate keeper of passage between the space of opportunity meeting obstacle. He tends to grant passage to those who possess knowledge that can be useful, a token or treasure of value as trade, or

soul for trade. He is rumored to allow the Nero people passage more frequently when accompanied by a soul that is of Elbrus lineage. He also has the ability to see your intentions and allow passage based on agendas alone.

He has often had more encounters with Nero than any other group in America. Barry was a determined businessman. His purpose was to give his people the sound they wanted. The sound of soul from an instrument. The artists formed from Barry were blessed by Aria. No other God who favored musicians could denounce souls that were under Aria once she favored them. Barry began to produce male singing groups. This was modeled by him observing Oculus blueprint. When Aria noticed Barry off the beating path, she would sometimes come to visit him. Mostly in the form of an older women resembling his mother. Aria offering a thought, "Do you believe yourself to be a duplicate? You follow a blueprint that is not exclusive to your people. Oculus is a God of old ways. It is your duty to show the way of the *new*, the Nero way!"

Aria continues, "What you think you see is profiteering, but in all actuality, Oculus and many of the Elbrus Gods, showcase the young males to communicate globally to other Gods who show interest in young boys for their own sexualized agendas. I implore you Barry, you have no direction to travel except forward. Be the trailblazer you were destined to be." Aria was always invited to mortal affairs, she casually would show with servants, devotedly massaging her vocals, periodically feeding her sliced lemon. While up north, Droger, the God of Perseverance and Drive, assisted Aria. Droger was a connoisseur of Aria's music. To promote her cause, he reached out to Geechee native Robert Abbott. Both esquire and editor, he held annual parades for the Nero's of the North. During the Bud Biliken Parade, many of her artist's believers stood in spectacle of her glory and the Demi-Gods and Icons she brought along.

Aria was personally invited to see Marilyn, one of the first Nymphs slaved under Heflin at his palace. Heflin, a Demi-God, master of manipulation and seduction. Also male nymph, Heflin was taught the dark enchantments from Cephalos himself. During this ceremony, many Gods were in appearance. One was Juniper, brother of Magnus, son of Potis. Junipers personality was an adult growing into a child. He sort out gossip and banter mostly.

Juniper, God of Sexual Journey, took a liking to Aria and her sisters many years ago after hanging around Etoile's offspring, Josephine Baker. He stayed around Etoile from time to time. Most of the information Etoile acquired of Gods and Goddess like Potis or Skadela or Drogheda, came from Juniper himself. Magnus was also in attendance, only as a guest and not a soldier, so he did not combat with any Nero Gods.

The Goddess Chera was also invited. Chera, was the daughter of a surrogate King. Oculus, also known as, Walking Eye, saw a prophet of a Goddess from the lands of Armenia and brought her soul to the new lands. Goddess of Popularity, she also commanded an army the size of a small state thanks to her father's connections as King. Chera often crossed paths with Aria and her siblings for centuries. Though she showed a warm exterior, Chera began to feel contrary emotions towards Aria at this celebration once seeing the young God, Barry. Many older Elbrus Gods feared the idea of Nero mortals possessing the ability to sway minds by sound, song, and melody. Chera knew this was the chosen one, a Nero Demi-God to orchestrate a new space for Gods to come.

Barry was Aria's plus-one to this celebration. Many Nymphs flocked to Barry. As protection, Aria placed a spell over him, a song to play in his ears to avoid the call of the Nymphs. The one thing she could not protect, was Barry interests in smoking. As Barry min-

gled, he noticed a seiza style smoking session and decides to join in.

Barry takes a pull and falls into an internal dream state. Still under the enchantment of Aria, a song still plays continuously between his ears. This metronome and cannibus combination, placed Barry in a trans-quantum state. Barry is then temporarily blinded from a shining light. A statuesque Goddess of bronze-golden skin begins to glow. She stood there, fierce, with a crescent shaped necklace and chest armor made of gems and shells.

As Aria notices the unbalanced Barry frolic around, Gods approach Aria. Aria looks over and smirks, "Ah Yes Chera! Here, hale, the Great One! Lord Barry!" Those around applaud. Chera replies, "Ah-ha, the honor is mine! The Great Barry! I see word travels rather swiftly, when I hear tales of a young one to bring about a great deal of followers to the songstress Aria!" Barry stares off into a daze trying to speak. He reaches his hand down to Chera's foot, mistaken it for her hand to shake. Aria pulls his hand back quickly from Chera, "I believe a bit too excited!- Rejoiceful even!- Meeting such rarity of Gods." Aria continues, "It's his first time around *Gods of Substance!*" Chera nods her in agreement and with a knowing as onlookers watched, she simply relies, "Yes, substance indeed!" As they passively evade more useless chatter, Chera concludes, "As you will excuse my presence is needed, you lovelies have a joyful night!" A strong scent of lavender passes the nose of Chera. It was Juniper, as he quickly grabs the Goddess, Etoile off to mingle. Juniper neglecting any form of discretion, seen courting with a Nero God in public was frowned upon. As Chera makes her way to Drogheda, she overhears her assisting Marilyn in a possible plan to flee the celebration. The reason in Potis using Drogheda's daughter, Aunjanue, to infiltrate the Nero God's believers in the later decades. Barry becomes slightly coherent and shocked in disbelief. Aria explains to Barry, "You saw my sister, Etoile, a Goddess in her own right.

In true form I might add! An impossible sighting for almost all mortals. She is notorious for traveling through realms. My promiscuous sister seeks the curiosity to be liked by many. She would become uninterested at times, operating on what a person will become rather than who they currently are." Etoile in all her flamboyance embraced those who shown self-interest, internally or external. Goddess of Style and Grace, Etoile was the most influential God for the Revolutionary Era. She often wore her hair in a short Afro or braids. Wearing a dress that was built as armor, her garments was forged by Darious, Lord of Craftsmanship.

Aria, was keen to when a welcome was worn out. She noticed the room of Gods beginning to feel a mortal cringe, as gossip began to spread about the agendas of Drogheda. Aria speaking with Heflin, "Your most gracious host, we shall be leaving now. The explosion of Nymphs have brought on a fatigue that needs healing." Barry, after seeing Etoile, made him want to change the direction of music. He wanted to incorporate more female musicians. During an audition with Barry, a woman comes into the studio, radiating a surge of confidence. *It was her*, well, at least that's what Barry thought for a moment, standing in the presence of a Goddess. Barry excited, playing it cool, "My, my, what is your name little lady...!?" She replies, "It's Diana." Her eyes were fierce and bulgy, her looked demanded you speak truth from your heart. Barry thought of Diana as the type of woman that should be the symbol of "beauty" due to her being the closest to resemble Etoile. Barry helped artists write songs about Etoile's essence.

Many artists under Barry, began to sing songs in praise of Etoile. Some artist received backlash from Aria if they were only creating a body of work just to seek praise from Etoile. As Barry passed down this message, many artists, singers, and musicians alike, began calling to Aria and other Gods they served. One song sung in praise to the City of the Gods, Tremé, was

from the music group, The Staple Singers. A tale of a place that's full of re-joice, excitement and worrisome. A place sung to the Nero people of American land, where there is a sense of Hope. Years followed as artists like Rose Royce would sing a tale of Etoile, titled, "Wishing on a Star," a song of praying to the Goddess in hopes of finding love. Etoile, in English translation, is a star-shaped being. The artist Stevie Wonder, though visually impaired, tells Barry in later years about his encounter with the Goddess, Etoile and how it inspired him to write the song, "My Cherie Amor." Aria appears to Barry and his artists on a night of a celebration. Champagne, fruits, jewelry, and even hair were gifts left to the Goddess when a mortal needed favor.

She gathers around them to leave them with a final message. "As you all are here, I want this to be heard. You are no longer poor. You are now rich! Rich not in terms of wealth but in spirit. This currency can allow you travel through worlds and time without being held by outside bias or boundaries. Even the God, Drahmen cannot interfere with such talents. Let my name ring true and build establishments in my name. I have made a promise to you all, that nor man, nor God shall deter you from greatness. I speak with a cautionary tongue! Do not allow any amount of money to rule primary! Make righteous decisions and let the music to your ears breathe life yet again!"

It began with the forming of fingers and toes. Hair full and golden with a shade the color of cinnamon. Eyes dark hazel. Ears small and large breast. These Hybrids or *Sloars,* are spawns of the Orcheus. A Spirit that breathes life through submissiveness. Known to the world as Nymphs, they were a second wave of Potis governed slaves. They were different from the previous, *Seducers.* They descend from the blood of Potis with the sperm of Aeoris and egg of Drogheda. They are most sexual and more dangerous. Unfazed by mortal pain and mortal judgment. They are nymphs that occur in the media realm. Dryden and Potis were some of the few Gods who built a tolerance for sex. Unlike traditional sirens or nymphs, they sung no song, nor cried a name. Skadela, a Goddess, who served as their liaison in many realms, connects them to souls who are lost and without emotional connection. They have the ability to transform and appear as regular mortal woman or men. They can camouflage between bodies and sometimes shape shift into animals such as hounds and birds. Aunjanue, Goddess of Youth, Naivety, and Rebellious, daughter of Aeoris was appointed leader of many Hybrids during their mission to dismantle Dryden and his followers.

Aunjanue was not just one race or one gender. She was supreme in every way. A shape shifter. She can be man and woman if needed. She was a caged Sloar. She was known in the mortal world for her sexual exploits through media. She was the first to introduce pornography to mortals during this time. Andren was primary in the start of this era for the Sloars. Andren, a Demi-God and the artist responsible for immortalizing the Goddess, Barbie and the late, Marilyn. He wanted to study the caged Aunjanue, for a portrait. Unable to capture her on a canvas from horrible lighting, he decided to film her. It was through film, her spirit of Sloar came alive. Many of the soldiers who stood guard and spectated Andren's experiment, were unable to resist the urge of her sexual allure. They begged Andren to partake in acts with her on film. Magnus, Potis' son, didn't like the idea of sex to be filmed

of Aunjanue due to his infatuation with her. He attempted to lay with her more than once but was rejected by her for his entitlement to her body. Aunjanue was also very loyal to her mother. Drogheda favored her more than anyone. She held a power to alter and change one's mind on command. The ability to enchant any man and even some Gods. Because of this, many Gods wore shields or cast spells on themselves to block Aunjanue's enchantments. Viewing her through a film however, was much more challenging to resist her. Many men were pulled to her and suffered declines in their libido. Mortal men fell into a dark spiral of no longer aroused by mortal woman causing a dysfunction in their relationships.

She found joy in the pleasure of manipulating a man's heart and his mind. Because of this, Potis kept her locked away in fear of luring his men to a sexual deadly fate. In her era of reign, many men's ego were tested in pursuing her. When called to, Aunjanue was released after Potis gained advisement from council of her usefulness for a potential battle. In her first days released, she is told to find the key to controlling Piruphius army. In doing so, she headed towards the Westlands. She often found distractions in night clubs. This is where she met a man, a fallen star of some sorts. His name was Rick. Rick was a young man exposed to Aunjanue at a young age. He would sneak into his uncles closet to grab tapes with her on it. Along with his curiosity followed an unguided journey of sexual expression. Rick was always flirtatious with the girls around his neighborhood, trying to explore his interest.

Going out to clubs and events, Rick started to date more women. Rick's actual girlfriend was a dark-skinned, long legged-incredibly patient bartender, who held a great relationship with Rick publicly. In private, Rick often created a feud with Robin, shouting, "Move your hips a bit baby! No baby, to the right! Ah, ah no, my right!" As the attempt for intimacy failed, his frustration rose, finding himself pull-

ing out a tape of Aunjanue to satisfy his desires. This also led Robin to believe he was cheating. An agitated Robin shouts, "We've never done that position before! I wonder what ho gave you that idea!" As an up-and-coming musician, Rick came into contact with many woman. By this time, Rick became a recognized musician. Goddess, Aria, began to favor his talents. If appearing to be a good image in her eyes, Aria would sometimes appear at an event with her mortal of interest. She invited Rick to an industry networking event.

As Rick navigates the room with Aria and her sister, Etoile, he couldn't believe who appeared in front of him. It was Aunjanue! He tried his best to not be that young boy, sneaking tapes from his uncle. He was now an Icon and wanted to impress a Goddess. He noticed Aunjanue did not appear to be the unibrowed, olive-skinned slim girl from the videos. "It's lovely to meet you," Rick speaks. "I've watched you my whole life. It's funny you seem taller on screen." As he continues his conversation, Rick noticed her date grew increasingly jealous. Aunjanue continues as her date flips out in a rage, as security removes him. She turns back looking at him while she waves him off smiling. Rick, while watching the man get dragged off, persist, "Look here baby, I've always wanted you…" Aunjanue speaks briefly, "Why thank you. I get that a lot! Look, I can't stay long, I been here too long already, maybe we can see each other later, I just lost my date, so I'm free!" Before leaving, both Goddess, Aria and Etoile privately chat with Aunjanue.

Aria speaks, "I understand what you are and I am aware of your commitments. I have no business to interfere. I show great favor to your mother. As a Goddess of many believers, I can hear some of them speak of a women who mastered the ways of manipulation. The moment I saw you, I knew you were who they spoke of." Etoile found Aunjanue promiscuous behavior enticing. "I like you, you're brave, many of us are seen as Sloars

to Gods when shown a side of sexual freedom. The mortals worship us, they are who serve us gifts and sacrifices more than any God has ever."

As they conclude the conversation, Etoile removes space between her and Aunjanue, discreetly whispering, "Here take this…" It was a piece of fabric with bullion embroidery that had the ability to change into baroque armor. "Wear this to protect your heart, no God or mortal or ghost or witch deserves to get close to you. Only when they've made a effort of true love and trade, shall you take this off." Gracious Aunjanue, calls back to Etoile to gift her as well. A metal comb made of brass. The comb was passed down from Drogheda and her ancestors when their hair would get wet or tangled. This comb would bring a great outlook to the hair of the Nero. When they scheduled a date, Rick noticed he wasn't as sexually excited. Rick tried to ignite his drive by rushing to the restroom to masturbate. Arriving back to the table tipsy, Rick couldn't find the right time to make his move, thinking to himself, "Should I touch her thigh? Should I slide over a bit more? Damn, maybe I should bulge my pants tighter!" His indecisiveness left him feeling hopeless. To cheer himself up, Rick decided to mingle with *regular* women. "Charlie make the left!" Rick shouted as he brought girls back to his place. The selection process was simple. Those who looked more of Aunjanue aesthetic, were the primary choice.

His direction for his music videos led to him taking out more Nero women and keeping those of lighter shade. Women would flock into Rick's love spell every night offering themselves to him. With no one being good enough, this led Rick to have a decline in his libido as well as his sanity. On a closing night of his concert, Rick screams in anger as the women he laid with, did not satisfy him. The two women jumped up out the bed to run outside the hotel room as security runs in. Seeing Rick in the chair naked watching a video in tears whispering, "Aunjanue."

Aunjanue moved along quickly, keeping her eye on the mission. Navigating the Westland terrain, she builds a team, the Hybrids. Hybrids appetite was constant and never fully pleased. They were glorified Icons and inspired mortals such as the Dawness of Porn, Lovelace. If Lovelace was the Queen of adult film, Aunjanue was shortly a Goddess.

With her Hybrids, it didn't take long to find the God of interest. He was sort of a gossiper and loudmouth. Tyrothion, a God of Rebellion (Alliance) and Expression, was son to Piruphius and Aria. He carried many women around and found pleasure in pleasing them. Tyrothion was built husky and displayed various metals and weapons that often-had unnecessary embellishments. When absent, his father left him in charge of the army in which protected Dryden's speakers. Tyrothion seen Aunjanue passing through his worlds. While around his disciples he begins to boast about his attempt to get any woman. Cat calling, he repeated more aggressive and greater each time. Sarcastic Tyrothion, "Well I finally land my sights on a Goddess amongst mere mortals! You need a God like me to complement your Aura!" Aunjanue responds smitten at the lack of difficulty to took to find him. Aunjanue is then aggressively pulled closer by Tyrothion.

They spent days in love. Tyrothion laying there in a mirage of thoughts decides to ask Aunjanue a question. "My love, I don't mean to be intrusive, I'm curious. How many souls have you conquered!?" Aunjanue looks over, "Why would you ask me that!?" Tyrothion regrets, "Love, My apologies, I didn't mean –" Aunjanue laughs, "I don't mind, it was a joke. I'm not sure, I have lost count. There in my home, I have a ledger to keep track of souls I've encountered, sexually." The Goddess and Tyrothion became casual, traveling together to several Panther meetings and Tribe gatherings. One in Northland at a rally held by Hampton, a co-leader of the Panther organization.

During these gathering, Aunjanue was adored by many Gods and men. Her next target was present, as she had her sights set on Dryden.

Aunjanue waited for the right moment to say something to him, "The great Lord Dryden! Have you decided to indulge me with a drink or two!?" Dryden looks on somewhat annoyed. "Young Mistress, the attempts you make are those of a mere youth. My mind, nor tongue shall indulge no further, now go! Go and appease me with your absence."

This was one of the few times Aunjanue was flustered. For no man or God has given her such dismissive approach. She stayed for a while, as Tyrothion introduces Aunjanue to his parents, Piruphius and Aria, and Aria's sister, Etoile, along with her lover. In a quick unnoticed glance, Etoile gives a wink to Aunjanue before introducing her mate. Etoile's lover was seen as weird and wasn't very formal. He was one of the older Gods who was an artist but fancied mortal men's tailored suits. He wore a steam blue pin stripe suit. With a hook attached to his right hand, he reached out to Aunjanue to greet her hand. Many Gods saw this as odd, seeing as Gods have no missing limbs. "Daninus is my name but call me *Candyman*. I am no God, but a Ghost-God. I cannot be harmed by a mortal or a God without proper spells from the Supremes, but that's neither here nor there!" Simultaneously to Daninus introduction, Piruphius whispers to his son of Aunjanue's treacherous ways but was met with ignorance and valor. An off put Tyrothion pulls Aunjanue back from the gathering and walks to see other guest. Piruphius sneaks off to address Aunjanue head on. Piruphius, in a small hallway, grabs Aunjanue from her neck demanding a response, "What tricks are you up to!" Pain was something she found pleasure in, so this wasn't effective. He then looks down, noticing Aunjanue is pregnant and decides to let her go. She looks up at him and replies, "He's going to be a great warrior like his father! I'm going to call him Damian!" Aunjanue felt a whiff of Pir-

uphius' aura grow with fire. Immensely strong, it cast a dazzle over Aunjanue, leaving her to submit to giving up Potis location. In doing so, he meets Drahmen. Drahmen, God of Adaptation, Obstacle, and Opportunity. He tends to favor mortal man that travel with a member of Elbrus bloodline. He lives between the space of opportunity and obstacle in the mortal world. Only when a man faces this moment, Drahmen appears weighing their intentions and worthiness, allowing them to pass or not. Casting judgment and intention of Piruphius action, Drahmen ask, "Why do you come?" "I see a moment to strike, Potis… he is at rest." Drahmen waves his hand under him to let Piruphius pass and suddenly, Drahmen grabs Piruphius from behind. Bending his right arm over his shoulder and choking him, Piruphius shouts, "Get your hands off me Drahmen!"

Piruphius turns to notice two heads. Known as Godly obstacle, it was Potis disguised as the God, Drahmen. Drahmen, was approached by Potis in advance, and so, he was given the blessing of opportunity to strike first. They scuffle for a moment as Piruphius calls on his hound Jaubauis to attack. "You think you can trust her!? Potis, shouts, "She can't be trusted, she told me you would be here!" Tussling with Piruphius, Piruphius breaks free and stabs Potis in the thigh as his hound jumps to bite Potis off of her master. Potis sends word to Magnus to prepare a thousand men to the Westland to prepare for war.

It was a slaughter. Men, women and children were killed. Magnus, loyal to his own, cleans up the streets flowing of blood and bones. Magnus seeing Aunjanue laying hurt and instead of picking her up he replies, "Why!? Why couldn't you choose me, you lay here with your decision. A decision to have a child with a Nero. You disgust me, you filthy Sloar!" Aunjanue somewhat coherent, wakes to see a large man with hair on his face, carrying her through a tan tinted sky. She doses back off to hear fighting in the distance until she finally falls fully unconscious. Aunjanue conva-

lescing, was healed by the all-powerful Josephine, a Goddess of Herb and Medicine. She was able to diagnosis Aunjanue, treating her with several minerals and stones to create balance in Aunjanue's lymphatic system.

Josephine's rule of healing was primary around the principals of balance. She often said, "What you place, you must unplace and when you take one, you must untake one." A remedy for the entitled who lack awareness or unawareness. Aunjanue went on to have several children with Tyrothion. Many of Aunjanue Hybrids fell to the feet of Tyrothion men. Some became prostitutes or escorts. Other Hybrids focus was to provide and serve Tyrothion and his empire. They were slaves he acquired and looked after when war was over and were left neglected by Potis and Drogheda. Many of them served and bathe Aunjanue. As turmoil between the Gods subsided, Aunjanue grew bored in the home of Tyrothion.

Gods gathered it was Taurean who kidnapped Aunjanue from Tyrothion. Taurean, God of Flamboyance, Swag, and Confidence, would come at a perfect time. He looked appealing to Aunjanue. Taurean was young and brandished markings of the mortal's text and art on his forearms and body. His teeth were replaced with gold. He carried himself with such bravado. Taurean was gifted an enchantment from his father with the ability to deflect Aunjanue's inheritable deadly persuasions. The spell also allowed Taurean to see with his eyes and ears. Never calling to her name, Taurean would be protected from her cunning spirit.

It was one of the smallest towns in America. Locals would have to travel to the next town for letters and groceries. This is where Marilyn and her family grew up. Her mother, half-sister and stepfather shared a small home. A one floor shack. Marilyn and her sister spent a lot of time together playing with dolls. Her hero was Barbie, Goddess of Du Jour, Vogue and Abundance. Given the opportunity, Marilyn would sneak into her parents' dresser drawer to play *Dress-Up*, wearing their mother's or even father's clothes and accessories.

During Marilyn's time by herself in the house, she'd model in the mirror with pearls and earrings with bras and lingerie. This was from finding posters and magazines featuring pin-up models and burlesque women. This stash usually sat beneath her father's clothes underneath a briefcase. Day in and day out, she prayed for such luck and blessing to find herself between a centerfold. Marilyn's mother and father began to have a chaotic and tumultuous relationship. Frank became abusive as time progressed, yelling and shouting making the home gradually unstable. Most of the arguments Marilyn perceived from her parents were in regard to her mother gaining weight. Eventually, Marilyn's mother grabbed the courage to leave him. In doing so, Marilyn would also have to part with her best friend, her sister. Marilyn and her mother moved to multiple cities before ending in the western lands. Her mother couldn't handle the transition of being a housewife to a working-woman. Her mother found herself in the pyschward after going through several spurts of depression.

"Do you know what love is dear?" Her mother would say this to Marilyn consistently. A bitter version of her mother would follow behind with "Never depend on a man darling, we don't need them!" Only a teenager, Marilyn bounced around several orphanage and foster homes. The more she traveled the less pieces of clothing she had. Her last piece of material left was a damp, rolled, pin up poster.

Preparing for a whole new world of high school, the girls and boys were a bit bigger and somewhat more social. Marilyn stayed to herself, making passive friendships as months passed. With only a few years left to graduate, Marilyn decided to leave to pursue her journey as a model. Marilyn became a small fish in a big pond, revolving through casting after casting during the Golden era of cinema and photography.

Leaving an audition, she stumbles onto a smooth-talking navy-man. He wasn't the most attractive, but his words made up for his looks. James courted Marilyn frequently as dates and cinema were a weekly thing. The relationship blossomed into a marriage. Following their honeymoon phase, Marilyn grew bored, feeling her true calling has gone astray. In her favor, James is called into battle during the Second World War.

This gave Marilyn an opportunity to navigate back in her path. She would find herself at the seventh street mall downtown trying on gowns, swiping dresses into her bag. She avoided asking James for money, knowing that questions would be raised. Marilyn snagged a few auditions. Sitting in front of a vanity mirror, she was hoping for this audition to work. She interlocked her fingers to pray, "Please God! Please! I need this to work. This is all I want!" "Ah, ahh, Norm… Nor-ma!?" The assistant fumbles through the name. Getting up from the seat, walking in the room, Marilyn replies, "Yes, that's me!" Walking in, she sees a man, long face, palms huge, clinching a lit cigarette behind a desk. He doesn't look up as he reads a magazine. Marilyn hands him some papers, running over her own words, "So here's my portfolio, I can dance a bit- I uh, I, I, I do- model-" The strange man responds, "-Don't sit, this won't take long! My name?" He laughs a bit, "You can call me Howard, but my friends know me as Potis" "Well, I can be your friend? Mr. Potis!" Marilyn gives a wink as they both chuckle a bit. Howard puts down his cigarette, "Look, let's get down to it all. We've been watching you for years. You're willing to do whatever it takes to get what you want, yea? Having said that, I'm curious to know your depth of dedication young Norma." She interrupts, "Ah, uh, you can call me Marilyn, my friends call me Marilyn!"

"Well, Marilyn, it's my job to let you know what you want! You want to be desired! You want a voice and to be taken serious! A world where you can say no without an explanation. Or better yet, a yes without giving one. What if I can give you that, what would you say!?" Howard stares directly at Marilyn. "Would you show your loyalty to me? Would you worship me!?" Marilyn compelled, lifted off her feet and pulled to the desk. Potis grabs Marilyn and turns her around forcing himself on her. A slow blow from Potis into Marilyn's ear, makes her submit. Marilyn unable to speak. Potis tilts her head back to his right ear, letting out a moan, "Potis!" From that day forward, she was given favor from Potis. Her first wish was granted, a pin-up featured on the first piece of *PLAYBOY*, setting the tone for woman to follow after her.

Seducers were the first established Orcheus under Potis. Orcheus were modern nymphs in the new land. Resembling phenotypes close to that of Drogheda, the Goddess of Seduction and Hunger, they had voluptuous breast with fiery-golden hair the texture of silk. Their skin was milky and physical traits appearing to mortals thin like the Goddess, Barbie.

The Seducers, existed in the realm through literature and/or photograph. Never quite could a average mortal access these women, Potis kept them for political and influential patrons. They were the gateway for him to obtain more power as a God in the new land. Getting more into the social life, the *Bunnies* praised Marilyn, hailing her as their superior. The Bunnies were Seducers, solely living in the House of Heflin, a Demi-God and offspring of Potis. He oversaw their wellbe-

ing and day to day lifestyle when Potis or Drogheda was not around.

It was everything Marilyn couldn't dream of. They brought her into the world, even deeper. A palace filled with wines and berries, jewels and servants and slaves. Hooch or drugs was often obtained from Weogufka, he was sort of a salesmen around this time but a God nonetheless. The more the woman consumed Weogufka potions, the more they would share sexual tales to one another. Mortals were slaves to these women if without caution. Ironically, these woman would be slaves to Weogufka, if not without the practice of the same preparations as their male counterparts. If disciplined, a Seducer, could extract almost anything from man. "I walked in this room, it was like they were under a trance, dispelling secrets and ideas to every woman who would pay them attention. After a while, it was hard to distinguish who was sharing more information, them or us. Weekends were more intense. Though rich and powerful, I've witness men who were on their third marriage with several amounts of debts and children, occupied the palace the most.

From time to time, celebrities and Icons would come to indulge. One lady, so gorgeous, her clothes looked like they were made of seashells. She was a Goddess, her name was Aria. Only a few Nero were invited but she surpassed racial barriers. When she spoke, it was like a song. Her voice delicate, graceful, and harmonic, levitating the room. She never stayed long in the palace and was usually there for introduction of a protégé or a project she was invested in. There would be a huge roar and stampede towards the front gates that were made of crystals. The Seducers would scream and fall to their knees in praise. The Goddess of Pop and Allure has arrived, and her name was Chera. She was the most divine being. I heard stories of her favored from Goddess, like Athena.

I couldn't believe it, slaves, servants, and patrons all yearning to savor an

ornament or stone falling from her dress as she climbs the palace steps." Chera speaks, "And you are!" "I stood there, in front of her, while Heflin introduces me. She raises her hand for me to kiss as I noticed a large ring made of stones. I kiss her hand looking up slightly with an innocence, simply, it's Marilyn". Chera giggles a bit embracing Marilyn. "The new prophet I hear, a Goddess in the making!" The two sit and talk for bit as Chera concludes, "Now if you'll excuse me, my presence is called upon." As Heflin pulls me back into the palace, I watch everyone gather, as I drift to the side. I then hear a call, a faint call. I looked to the corner to see a tall Amazonian woman introduce herself as Drogheda. She explains she is a protector of sorts, a Goddess of Pleasures and Hunger. Her look was tempting, even for a woman to fall. She had a hunger in her eyes and carried this spirit of being a socialite, while simultaneously, aloof.

Marilyn was overwhelmed, this *being* standing over her at least a whole foot taller. "I can hear your heart," Drogheda confesses. Marilyn expresses, "How!? But how can that be! I met a man preaching the same tale, a tale which led me *here*. He said he knows me and knows my ways. How can that be so!?" Drogheda speaking in a slight rush, "If this man is whom I think, it is Potis, God of Supremacy and Obese. He has heard your call as well. All Gods can hear prayers and can choose to ignore or accept those we favor and unfavored. There are occasions where Supreme Gods cannot hear at all, not because their inability, but because you simply aren't loud and consistent enough. Potis hearing you, has benefit for him. Potis reaching you first is simply him being opportunistic." Marilyn pleads, "I'm sorry… I was just a bored and lonely housewife looking to *make it*. I have no idea what this is. It is a lot for me I'm sorry!" A skeptical Drogheda responds, "Regardless of your deflections, I can see you wanted this more than you profess. You have my blessing and favor regardless and in time you will thank me! When you pray, you must

prepare as well. This is required of all mortals. A prayer is answered with the exchange of commitment. When ready, I will take you to see An-dren. He is a craftsman and painter. Only an artist, if blessed by a God, can immortalize humans. Through forms of portrait or film or song, this process will transcend your spirit. You will be able to roam through-out worlds; influence and indulge worldly things. You must keep this to a secret. If he were to find out your betrayal to him, it can be fatal."

Having not been home in years, Marilyn returns to piles of letters. One letter reading a divorce from her former husband sent several months pri-or. As Marilyn's career excels, she soars into Icon status. Not a peep from Potis, until a ceremony where Seducers were given awards. Portraying as a Bunny, turned Actress, Skadela, Goddess of Disguise and Facade, is called on to instruct Marilyn of her next steps. Slipping a note under the table for Marilyn to read, "...from Josephine: small dose, nothing more!"

After leaving the event, Marilyn heads to her room, seeing a bottle on the dresser. Knocking at the door, Potis son, Magnus informs Marilyn of her objective. "He was a married man, I knew that much walking into the sit-uation. He carried himself in public with a really cool and calm demeanor but in private was quite an asshole. We spent weekends on a yacht with his brother. As I found out much later, the yacht belonged to his wife. I believe she knew, but never allowed such humiliation to surface publicly." More often than not, they spent their time intoxicated. Marilyn frequent the use of Josephine's concoction. Infiltrating an offspring of Potis, she was able to record and relay messages back to Magnus of their plans. In these recordings, Potis was satisfied with the news Marilyn presented but grew cautioned of her after she carelessly divulged the agendas of Potis to John during a session of Marilyn and John pillow talk. Marilyn was now seen as a threat. In an attempt to flee, Magnus kidnaps the Demi-God-

dess, injecting her with a fatal dose of the drug she received from Josephine. That night, Drogheda mourns the death of Marilyn in the physical form. With a portrait created from Andren, the blood of Marilyn and the use of a resurrection spell, Marilyn is reborn, living amongst the inspired.

There was an abyss of emptiness in the middle of the Southland. Nothing sat between the crossroad except a railroad track and a neglectful bench. Quite some ways away, a man is called upon in a whisper. He is asked to bring items. This walk cost him a full day of labor and rest. As the man approaches the crossroads with a guitar and a small bag, the Sun was hitting its lowest point before finally allowing the Moon to take it's place. He sees a goat approaching in the distance.

The goat, small but somewhat stout, arrives closer, walking with a slight limp. Robert thinks nothing of it at first. Suddenly he hears a voice, "So did you bring what is needed!?" Robert looks up stunned, not sure if he heard correctly, a goat talking. Robert looks up to the sky yelling, "It is you, Oh! Is it you Legba!? My eyes aren't that good these days, but is it true, have you returned to me!?" The goat chuckles, "No, I am not the Mighty Legba! If I may ask, your guitar? Can I see it!? Do you know a few tunes on this thing!?" The goat gives a soft headbutt to the guitar. The goat speaks again, circling the man, "You know the song, *Love in my Veins*, it was a song I recited to myself many times, do you mind playing it for us!?"

Robert begins to play, even with a rusty and broken guitar, it didn't stop his instinctual musical abilities. The goat kicks his hind legs out in rejoice. The goat, then stops his dance, as he becomes irritated, noticing that a few pegs needed tighten. "You are truly extraordinary Sir-Robert... May I !?" The goat forms a human chest, torso and arms along with a human head. In his changing, Robert looks up dropping his guitar to the ground. The beast picks up the guitar to tune it. He pulls out a cowrie shell he kept on his earring and uses it to clasp one of the strings back to the brigade of the guitar. He flickers some of the strings. Looking back at Robert, he asks again, "So have you brought what is needed?" Robert shakes his head rushing to hand over the bag. In the bag,

was a cane plant, water, a large cloth, and cotton flower. The beast uses the cloth and water to subdue the scar and injury on his face. The sugarcane was used to numb the pain. Before returning the guitar, he stuffs the cotton in the sound hole for percussion.

Handing back the guitar, he says to the man, "My dear son, my name is Piruphius, Lord of Unity, Assembly, Resilience, and Strength, I have called on you and you've answered and you have shown loyalty." While listening, Robert received a newly restored guitar. "As a God, I shall grant you blessing and favor. Being in a Gods' favor Robert, your guitar can be heard far and wide now, even by other Gods whether they support or oppose your call. Return home now, I send you as a messenger. The Goddess, Aria, will now hear your calls and prayers. Return with the song in mind, *Honey Blues*, play in the musical note A and she will know who has sent you."

Robert returns back to his family on the plantation. The neighborhood gathers around daily to hear him play. "That *Peruphius* was correct!" Robert said to himself, as the guitar played as if it wasn't a day old. The sound was magical and now Robert's soul was transformed through the sound of his guitar. Also there on the plantation, was a young Elbrus family. Their fate led them to the plantation to pay off a debt. A *debt* in the form of servitude quite different than their Nero counterparts. The Elbrus family owed to their Lord and God of the Southlands, Cephalos.

A little boy of the family, Sam, absorbed Robert's tunes, listening to the Nero spirituals. Inspired, Sam joined in on their spiritual gospels. Robert, though in favor of his supporters, did not like Sam or his family. One quiet night, he played the tune Piruphius mentioned. In A minor, he played all night calling to the Goddess, Aria. During Roberts call, he grew thirsty, making his way to the well. There at the well, stood a group of women.

Somewhat in tribal clothing, one turns to him, "That's a lovely guitar." Robert replies looking off to the side, "Why thank you mam." She begins to speak on things only Robert would know. "So ever since you've made a bargain, you're playing better now." Prying some more she asked, "I hope it was worth it! Robert responds, "Worth what!?" The women replies, "Your soul Robert, trading your soul." He looks on disturbed, "Look now mam, I don't know who you are and what trouble you gone cause, but I best be on my way back." The lady approached him, consoling his wrist, "No trouble is caused on my end. It is *I*, that knows the tune itself and who has sent you to play it. I have only sung that song to one."

He stops his movement, the women around her begin to carry her hair and oil her skin as she stands poise. Puzzled, yet, the remaining confident Robert speaks, "How do you know of this!? I reckon that trade was worth it. I have nothing else but my music. I live it! That trade seemed about fair to me mam." She smiles, "Yes, commitment to your passion is what I favor, but not obsession of it, my dear." Aria lifts Robert's head from the ground's direction responding, "I am Aria, Goddess of Song, Harmony, and Nurture. You've called to me, your fingers and instrument is mighty and just!" Excited Robert replies, "Oh yes! Mam Aria, you are the one he mentioned, "A great love he called you." Aria chuckles, "Yes, he would say!" Robert flips his guitar towards the front and begins to play for the Goddess sitting on the well. Closing her eyes reminiscing, Aria speaks. "Yes, this is what we would dance to before the war. Your trade was righteous, I shall offer you my blessing as well." Aria gifts Robert the ability of healing. As she gets up, her servants follow behind, she looks to Robert, "Now, what is a favor in return I shall grant you, young man?" He looks and ponders, "Well there's a family on the croplands, they watch, they study us, study our ways. I hate it Mam- I mean your Goddess!" Aria replies, "You speak of the young Elbrus boy! Your voice is no lon-

ger from your body, your voice is the vessel of your strings, sound, and soul. There will be many you shall infect. Many white, yellow, and brown youth and adults will heed your calling. The young child shall not be harmed. He is a believer of you and the culture, therefore he is a believer of me. There is also the factor of, they too, have their own deities they believe in. It would be a disservice to myself to harm a mortal believer. My Godly mistake will create a mortal punishment for a believer like you."

Aria continues, "I want you to remember, in a place of pain and anguish, your sound will bring healing to your people and people around. A tragedy, music cannot live or serve it's purpose unless performed. Do not be afraid of those who choose to replicate from your work. It is a gift and your gift has the ability to affect all. They will always need your guidance of pure inspiration to follow behind. I shall let him be, no loss shall come on to him nor anyone who is inspired by you, that is my favor to you. Your voice will live through them for eternity as you are a true pioneer."

Aria placed an enchantment to cultivate comprehension. As Robert builds comprehension, he responds, "I understand my Goddess. Before I depart, your lover gave me this." Robert takes his hat off and hands Aria a note saying, "The Circle." Two of Aria servants were sent to find Piruphius. Aria figured, Piruphius was back in the City of Gods, Tremé. A servant of Aria, finds him and returns with an update, "He's hurt, a wound of his is taking long to heal. He's home, he has requested you to see him."

Aria arrives to the City of Tremé. The oldest city for Nero people to find peace and tranquility. It was where the Supreme Goddess Eve, first settled. The city was home to many Gods. Dryden, God of Literature and Word, Lufkin, God of Guidance and Orizah, Goddess of Nourishment. Aria called to Orizah and Josephine to assist. Healing Goddess,

Orizah provided nourishment, such as rice, wheats and berries as Josephine, Goddess of Herb and Medicine healing, provided spiritual and immortal treatment. Aria sees him with his eyes closed, laying on his bed, hand on his chest next to the potion Josephine has given him.

Aria removed the cloth from Piruphius face to reveal a bullet the size of a grape pierced into his jaw, resting inside a tooth. Orizah was there to provide provisions for the God while also providing spiritual healing. She was also able to send servants to bathe Piruphius and assist him with meditation and resting of his soul. Piruphius convalescent for a total of three Godly days and nights, which was about 28 days to a mortal. Aria comes to him in the night, seeing him awake. Aria speaks softly, "I gather your mind is winding it's gears steadfast." Piruphius replies, "I had a vision of a fish. I wonder what it means. Could this be a vision from Lord Lufkin?" Aria concurs, "Ahh yes! Steadfast indeed." She walks toward him, holding him from behind, both standing on the balcony. She responds to the question, "Perhaps it's the trout Orizah has prepared! Maybe it could be the stream of catfish that frolic throughout the Bayou."

A combative and irritated Piruphius responds, "Aria! Or maybe it is truly a dream of a fish! A symbol! This is the very reason our love clashed. Why isn't your first thought to simply believe in my dream!" A sarcastic Aria replies, "Yes, you're right! How could I forget!? A fish offering from the fellow Gods!" Piruphius turns to her in a shout while Aria calms his emotions quickly with a hug. When Gods would hear Aria sing during their ceremonies, Gods would shed tears of joy in spectacle as they marvel at her holy tunes. She sings to him, laying him down, he smiles in reply, "Our mortal man has delivered both our calls." She looks down rubbing her fingers along his skin and rolling a stone of jade across his face then massaging her hands through his hair. As Aria concludes the song, Piruphius dozes off into a Gods nap.

Piruphius awakes with his wounds healed right on time as Aria returns with her servants. A teasing Aria continues in a laugh, "Thee old mighty one, finally awake and showing a slight glow of love, my apologies King, for such sarcasm was not needed on my end earlier." Piruphius smiles, "Oh yes you are always forgiven, but I too need to ask for forgiveness due to my shortness of temper." A servant rushes to their chambers, panting, demanding to speak with the Lord Piruphius. "Lord, there is an urgent message from Lufkin!" As Piruphius makes his way to the courtyard, seeing Lufkin, he warns him Aeoris has been spotted around the grounds of the city.

Potis, the God of Superiority and God of entitlement, sent his trusted beast, Aeoris, a American Pigeon gifted with gold feathers. Aeoris returned to Potis informing him of their exit from Tremé. Potis then makes a decision to send his clan. They weren't the most stealthiest of warriors and often gave their position away by wearing bright white clothing over their heads and bodies. Piruphius returns, as Aria sees him gathering his belongings. An Agitated Aria shouts, "Ha! Just as I suspected, only here for thy self!" Piruphius grows unsettled, "The problem is Potis is near. My Love! For once form a thought other than a defensive one!" Aria rises from the bed, "My defensiveness lies in the space of your needs conjoined with my remedies. You do not need to leave, we have more than enough believers here!"

An impatient Piruphius, "Yes, believers! Not soldiers, Love! It is not their responsibility to fight this war between Gods. The Elbrus Gods see us Nero Gods as a disturbance of their goals. I need to head north. Come with me my love. There are plenty of potential believers where I need to head. My brother is waiting for me." Piruphius continues his persuasive monologue convincing Aria to come on this journey. Many of Aria's followers offered to join them, even though a mortal's journey towards the North was much slower. Aria brought with her a personal pianist and critic. Pi-

ruphius, for an offering of the North, brought with him a collection of artifacts, furs, gold coins and metal, and art given to him from his people.

Building a comfort in their journey, Aria requests her Pianist, Iphris, to play music. Piruphius wakes up during their chariot ride, wiping his eyes. "I didn't mean to wake you," a relaxed Aria apologies. The pianist plays a note as Piruphius looks to Aria and smiles. "Now... I see you fully!" Piruphius shouts, "Hey, Iphris! Start from the beginning again!" He listens again to the music, as Aria grows a childlike embarrassment, hiding herself under Piruphius armpit. "What's this urge to run from your own body?" Aria peaks up with a reply, "...because now... You see me! You see me with this song, I wanted to write something for you." She then shouts, "Iphris! Please dear, would you play that one more time!" As Iphris replays the song, Aria duets, as Piruphius looking on to Aria, speaks, "Your soul is so beautiful!" As she finishes the song, they both shout to Iphris again, "Ok, play it one more time!"

The land was primarily of soil farmers and natives who followed the trails of livestock for food or warmth. The Gods of the native were strict on not letting other Gods or their believers pass through. The Gods of these lands were known as, *Keepers of the Eastern Door.*

To the Mohawks, the mortal natives that governed the land, were aware of the threat that Potis and his siblings were beginning to inflict. The issue that laid was miscommunication and entitlement of what belonged to who. Cayuga Lake was where most cattle such as deer, bear and fish arrived for rejuvenation. This lake at one time led to Lake Ontario, a lake connecting an outside land to the America. Potis wanted pure ownership of this land for the sale and trade of goods and services for his believers. With warning, he approached God Okwiraseh, one-half of twins who was in control of the section and grandchildren to the supreme Goddess, Lotsitsisonh or known to the Frenchman in Ontario, as Sky Woman. The Mohawk Gods spoke exclusively in their own language and with many of their unique gestures and tones. Potis took this as a sign of disrespect. Before the hasty action to react, he went to the Land of Nero to consult a translator. His offer was to give land for selective Nero. The God of Language, Dryden, was a Nero God and mastered years in translating language for Nero natives who were transitioning from language of the Congo and Cameroon to that of the Dutch, French and English.

Arriving to the north required much approval from Native Gods. Even Gods had to return with a peace offering for reentry. Dryden decided to bring with him four essentials to the natives. The first, was Orizah's dish, a food offering that consisted of chicken, sweet potatoes, steamed rice and a fish from the lakes of Tremé. The second, was a gift from the sister of Aria, Etoile's cloth, a linen and woven pants. The pants were something the Mohawks began to wear often and embellish their own

Tribes symbols and embroidery. Following, was a instrument made from the Nero people of the Southlands, a peace drum named Djembe. Lastly, was the language of the Nero people. This help build a foundation for the future relationships between Nero and natives. Dryden seen this introduction as a window of opportunity to develop his passions.

Gaining reentry to the lands of the north, Dryden holds a council with the Twin Gods in establishing a correspondence. In the north for a ceremony of the Mohawks, he was gifted an introduction to a Goddess by the name of Florence, she was a Native God who had the ability to bring breath to plant and soil throughout unfurnished land. She was quiet, her words were short and concise, she was a Goddess of Absorption and desired proper nurture. She was a God who was impressionable. Whatever she exposed herself to, could affect her overall growth as a Goddess. Dryden grew a strong fondness for Florence. Dryden saw the Goddess as a flower that needs to be treated with a respectable sense of responsibility and commitment. They started a exclusive relationship as Gods and developed a translation of love within the land of the North. Florence was held to the commitment of the north. She was the Goddess that provided substance to the Mohawk natives. Potis during these treaties grew impatient. Dryden's time in the land also adopted a relationship with the Twin Gods grandson Flint. Along with Flint, Dryden met his daughter Josephine. She was the Goddess of Herb and healing for Gods. She traveled close by Dryden side for years as he showed her a world outside the north, along with her son, Weogufka, a Demi-God who often experimented with his mothers elements to share with mortals.

Dryden's connection with the natives allowed a treaty of the supremes to have access to the Hudson River and rivers along the coast to Canada. As the treaty progressed, Potis followers decided to follow the ways of Dryden, they offered food and cloth to the Mohawks. What the natives

didn't know was the cloth and gifts that were offered from Potis and his mortals were rigged with infectious and poisonous disease. The Mohawk Tribes that lived near the borders were murdered of a slow death from these *gifts* from Potis people. Side effects of sickness, fatigue and even child defect, caused a war waged against the Natives and Elbrus Gods.

While this war began to brew, Dryden felt the decision to stay neutral was a smarter choice. During his stay in the north, Dryden business was of worldly things. Dealings throughout the galaxy and comprehension; psychology studies and behaviors. Dryden began working with universities and organizations. Potis grew angry with Dryden. "This was not a place for you to rest and build, I asked you this favor- in return, I bring you a small portion of the land for your people." Potis continues his rant as they gather in a courtyard of Dryden's home. "You benefited in every way, they were willing to share the land with you." Dryden continues. "Your ideology to rid them of their land has given you a strong sense of entitlement to something that doesn't belong to you. My answer remains, I do not go to war for the blood of mortals, that do not belong to the Nero's. Potis displeased, leaves the quarters without a word heading back to the Southlands. As the time moved on, Dryden noticed the land aged vacant of soil and plant life. The ground began to dry out. The seasons changed but took longer to return to a tropical state.

Dryden searched in numerous places for his love, Florence but was met with no luck. Dryden sought out the Gods of the Mohawk. During the conversation, it was Josephine's son who appeared detailing that a God of *pale shade* has kidnapped the Goddess, Flora. Dryden decided to go with Weogufka, a native cousin of Florence, to find her. He wasn't always one of the most sober Gods, closely connected with the vices of mortals. This relationship with mortals allowed Weogufka to tap into a community to help Dryden find Florence much faster.

Cephalos was a God who didn't come to the North which explained why most slaves were in the South. His power and control was at its strongest there. The further the Nero man went from Cephalos, the more their mind formed independent thought. Being in the Southlands without protection, Dryden felt he had to speed up his search, as Florence was the most gullible of most Gods, possibly becoming influenced by Cephalos' purpose. During his stay in the Southlands, Weogufka was able to bridge a relationship with a warrior God, Damu. He roamed the lands with his Tribe. They mainly lived in small cities and made a life off protecting other Nero and Tribes from abuse or danger from outside Gods and Lords. Damu enjoyed Weogufka company, eventually leading to Damu interactions with Dryden. As they sit and talk, Damu professes, "Lord Dryden, we know of his son, the one Abraham, he is an allie to us. He speaks on building a community for some of the Nero. He may lend a hand in this pursuit."

Abraham was fond of the Nero, especially Nero Gods and their ways. He was sort of a pre-hipster and pioneer of the idea of moving Elbrus mortals into the same neighborhood as Nero. However, he still wanted the Elbrus to have clean water and access to cattle. Upon arriving to Washington, Abraham embraces Dryden. Serving wine and poultry, "I see your trail for miles," Abraham humors Dryden, as he notices Dryden's stardust. A trail or path Gods often leave behind, when moving at a fast rate of speed. Dryden calms himself as Abraham explains, "He is a father of mind, but I only know this much about him. He is a God of Control, a God of Mindache, yes!? Dryden interrupts, "-Of course! I am aware, but I am also aware of his limitations. I heard stories of Cephalos where his travel is limited to the, *Line of Boundary.*" Abraham confirms, "Correct! However, it is not that he cannot leave, it is his choice to stay, simply because the soil is the strongest below the Line of boundary. This soil is key for domination, not just in American land. I've witness my own father turn Gods into ideas,

nymphs into his weekend pleasures and mortals, invisible to the world. Trust and believe, his decisions are more of a choice, than circumstance."

As he continues, "I understand that Florence possesses one ability to bring forth growth amongst the soil. My prediction is my father is looking to expand and needs a Gods blessing to the land." Dryden speaks aloud a thought. "That explains Potis persistence for the North merger. They never wanted to create a bond, they wanted possession." "Precisely!" Says Abraham. "Now I know the worlds are changing, I see a future, where your people don't show a fear for me, but a love. I've been working with a Goddess, Libertas, she is arriving to the lands soon and we are looking for you to be an ally on this. I have been given the sight of guide and path, Lord Dryden! Your people will need a place to stay when this is over. They will have a community, small shops and parks, and gospel. A culture they can cling to. I have the strategy to release them from the hold of my fathers choker." As their conversation develops, Dryden pauses Abraham, "A moment… I hear something! A whisper! My apologies, continue." Abraham, excited about his vision continues, "I need them to fight for me against my father. The Nero slaves! Damu's brother has already agreed to lead the battalion. If you can see this Dryden!? Florence returned and the Neros are free!"

Dryden with understanding, "I have seen this concept before. From you and your father and his father before, using my people to build!" A empathic Abraham, "This sight was given to me by Lufkin, you know of him, correct?" Dryden ponders, "Lufkin, you say?" "Yes, Lord of Guidance and Seeking," Abraham speaks, "I gather you crossed each others paths at one point!?" A retiring Dryden responds, "No Abraham, I gather your assumptions are based on our shade and not our endeavors. As Dryden stands up, "I have to table this proposal, I felt I was sitting with a being of a Gods mind, not a mortal-" Suddenly, Dryden jolts out of Abraham's chambers, fleeing,

leaving glass shattered and furniture tossed around. Within a blink of an eye, Dryden appears a moment after his son, Taurean, arm is sliced clean off! Dryden pulls a blade, of a birds beak, from his cloths. Fighting off Cephalos, Dryden and Cephalos tussle, as Damu arrives to assist Dryden. After the brief brawl, Dryden lands to see Florence clinched against Taurean's fingertips. Kneeling down, Dryden whispers softly, "Are you hurt my love?" Florence, trying to wiggle her way out, "No, no harm has come to me until your son's ways of manipulation caused for me to be trapped". Dryden stands up confused, "But, but, what and how did you get here! Dryden demanded, nervously. Florence forfeits trying to release herself, "My love, I came willingly. No God or man has ever stopped to care of what brings me life, but consistently request me to give that very life. My father nor my love have conjured a thought of compassion and empathy of my needs. Do you know what brings me life! The fragrance of magnolia, Cephalos presented this gift to me in return I bring life to this land." Dryden steps back, frustrated but comprehensive. With no words, Dryden says his goodbyes to his love as he leaves back to the North. Right before he takes off, he notices a young man who was tempted by Taurean ways. A young man named Norman. When asked, Dryden simply tells him, you've earned the arm of a God along with a Goddess who grants life to soil you have earned the right to do what you please.

In anger, Dryden carrying his son, Dryden scolds him, "Stay out of mortal affairs!" A wounded Taurean questions, "Father, they adore us, why can't you embrace this fact!? They are the reason we breathe. Your tunnel vision will cost the lives of many Nero to suffer!" As Dryden and his son travel back to the north, he arrives to the capital of the land to notice a large statue erected. Wounded Taurean replies, "Is this the makings of Potis or Cephalos, how could this be!? A statue of the one called Abraham? I don't understand!" Finally arriving to the north, Dryden returns home for his son to rest.

As he walks along the land, Dryden hears a crowd shouting louder for a being named Harriet. "Whom are we rejoicing," Dryden appearing as a young man asking a crowd participant. "It's Harriet, the Goddess of Freedom," says an older male. "Wait, what did this person do," envious Dryden speaks. "These are slaves, Harriet followed a path down to the Southlands and made her way back here, where we are *truly free*! What's wrong with you son! She's a Legend." Dryden breaks out in frustration, "Who is this Harriet!?" The older male jumps back, "Oh it's you!?" Seeing Dryden's charm hanging from his neck, "My apologies Lord Dryden!" Dryden replies, "I demand answers, who is this mortal being praised in my home! The older male replies cowering, "She found us Lord and helped us escape. She mentioned, she was given a path blessed by a God. The path showed her a new home. Dryden replies, "This is my home, my land, my name, you dear worship a mortal in my presence! The path that was given to her, was that of my own stardust-an accidental blessing!"

The old male continues, "Lord Dryden, she found us, we called for you, for years, some witnessed to have seen you years ago, during Cephalos' reign. Heavenly Lord, forgive us, we know you are the King of Ithaca, but Harriet is King now Lord, the people cry to her in rejoice. Please lord, let her rest in your home of Gods, she has meant no harm!" Dryden stands mighty, unsure of the punishment to inflict as the older male bows and speaks. "Dear Lord, we ask for forgiveness, we were slaves and had no knowledge that we were living in confusion to begin with." Dryden responds, "Now young Nero, my temper may have gotten the best of me, I am confused myself, I had no idea of this happening journey for you and the fellow Nero. Now lift your head and go rejoice." The older male, excited of the mercy from Dryden leaves, but before walking away, he looks back towards Dryden and replies, "Lord Dryden, I have a gift that was to be preserved for you to have!" It was a book, titled, "Language of the Nero by Norman."

Many of the Nero slaves were held by Cephalos. His mastery was control of the mind and sometimes the body but he could not master the soul. He then figured to do so was to immortalize his sons on currency. This tactic, maximized the potential over souls. Cephalos predicted to Gods, that this model will place a hold on his *cattle* for years to come. Many Nero will want to leave their own communities in disgust of their own people. Portray themselves as better or indifferent and even change their physical appearance for Cephalos' sons acceptance. However, outside of Cephalos mind grasp, his biggest triumph was the control of Flora. The Goddess of (Plant) Life and Soil.

She was captured from the Neros and placed into soil to produce food and resources for the Nero slaves to pick from for Cephalos and his sons. One slave who was a craftsman, impressed Cephalos and his men due to his skillfulness of flower picking. Norman, was the leader for picking cotton, berries, and wheat. He was a quick learner and faster instructor when showing new slaves how to pick. Norman was one of the few slaves who also profited off picking large quantities for Cephalos. He was gifted small amounts for his personal collection. He started to make garments and even dye them, changing the color and texture.

At times, the Goddess, Etoile, was pleased with Norman's clothing. Disguised as a slave, she wore some of his clothing for Sunday service. This day was when Cephalos would bring his best-dressed slaves to their religious ceremonies. Norman would show up to the field bright and early. His drive was unmatched, working around many Nero who passed out from lack of energy. At the height of Norman's work ethic, many of the Demi-Gods and Nero mortals did not like Norman's ability to thrive through the chaos. It made him appear to be a God. Norman never showed a moment of weakness or questioning. This presented a dilemma. Cephalos believed the slaves among Norman would see him as a pillar and the stron-

gest who can go against the machine that Cephalos himself have created. They believed due to his lack of fear, Norman's spirit will breed future slaves much more resilient. There was not much convincing Bojack, he was the overseer for the slaves within the plantation. Cephalos casted a dark spiraling thought over Bojack, making him feel as if Norman will take his position as master overseer. Standing some feet from the field, Bojack in anger, "Look at this Nigga, how tha fuck he think'd he best'd!? He think he'a want my spot, ya hear me! He wants my spot!" With Bojacks uproar, many of the subservient Neros fell into agreement of his statements. As the anger increased, Norman's focus prevailed. A slave in the field hints to Norman, "Hey the Sun is hotter today, so the wheats may burn." Norman replies, "Ain't no fear of others gonna deter me!" Many slaves began to chime in, "Yeah! He thinks he better than us!" Wearing his hair that way and out picking eerbody! Who the hell he get off, showing off!"

This made them more frustrated. Some slaves even began to sabotage some of the fields soil to get Norman in trouble. At the pace and momentum he was operating, this had very little affect. Though many of the slaves used tactics to rid themselves of Norman, it was Norman's own doing of praise to a being name *Dryden*. "Dryden, Thank you, Lord," Norman would sing his name while working in the field. On that night, Bojack and a few other slaves dragged Norman from his feet out of his shack across the gravel. Norman clothes ripping against the twigs and thorns, as he tries to get his balance all the while screaming. "We've had enough of your nonsense Norman, you think you better! You think you all high and mighty!" As the slaves grab rope and wrap Norman against a tree, the adults send the children to run to get more candles to gain better vision. Bojack grabs the first whip and cracks it against Norman's back. Many slaves begin to take turns, as Norman's flesh opens up. He doesn't cry, but yells out again, "DRYDEN!" Bojack in anger, grabs the whip back from a slave and releases a large lash against Norman

back, instantly breaking the tree in half, as Norman falls to the ground. The sons of Cephalos decided to let Norman lay convalescent on the ground for several days. Children of the slaves, periodically, would sneak Norman water and small rations of bread and berries. Once Norman bettered himself, he was met with more punishment for not picking in the field for the days missed. Cephalos and his sons condemned him to pick overtime, having him pick with a canteen at the peak of night. Norman, after fulfilling his debt, became less controversial and more conforming. Norman decided to fill his days with small talk and similarities with his slave mates. He often would say, "Man, it's gonna be a hot day today, it's gonna be hard out there!" After a few months, the slaves took a liken to Norman after his new found pessimistic ways. Within a year or so, Norman became somewhat a motivator, pushing his fellow slave mates towards spiritual healing. Norman was not an idiot, he knew he had to build a rapport with his peers to gain their trust. It was then, they heard Norman's words as similar and agreeable, rather than obnoxious and disconnected.

During a Sunday service, Norman was in prayer with several older slaves and young children. He opens his speech, "I know many of you took seasons to see me in your favor. I think what many of you haven't seen was who has had my favor. The Lord, Dryden, the Spirit of Language… he has shown me a way your Gods don't. You see! Cephalos and many others force their agenda and ideas and their Gods on us. Dryden is here for us all. All Neros who walk these lands. The ability to adapt and learn. The gift of comprehension. His words keep us in spirit of perseverance from the scorch of the Sun and heat of the gravel. Granted by *our* Lord." As Norman prophetess the knowing of Dryden, he starts to create bodies of work in the name of Dryden. Norman writes a secret book, titling, "Language of the Nero: Dryden." A book describing the tellings of the language and communication of the Nero people who have adapted

from Kikongo; Bantu language and Celtic languages. Slaves weren't allowed to read or write in their language or even the language of Cephalos and his followers. Norman began gaining slaves trust, leaving symbols and words from the book on small plants with berry juice and mud.

One evening, Cephalos' son sees a marking left on one of his child's clothes. The marking was a symbol from the boy's mother, who was a Nero Slave. She left a symbol of a sign of love on his shirt. George storms out the house demanding Bojack make an example of the mother for attempting to read and write to their son. When strapping the mother against a tree for punishment, she is given five lashes from each slave. Norman, onlooking, devastated, runs over to the crowd trying to bring them to a peaceful harmony. He shouts, "You see, we are property here! *HE* would not let us harm our own brother, mother, sister or kin. I ask you to call on to him. Dryden! Dryden! Norman goes to check on the mother the next day.

As he enters the shack, her back showing no more bruises or lashes as if it never happen. Norman runs outside in rejoice, calling all, "LOOK! Look what Lord Dryden has done! Let's call to him again to thank him!" They called to Dryden for days to give thanks after the Nero slave mother was healed. One night, a storm comes to the land during the midday. A bull, overly larger and clearly misplaced, comes throttling through the edge of the plantation where Norman would go to sneak to study. Norman looks up, shocked, as he backs up warning the bull not to approach. "I am Taurean!" The bull speaks, "I heard your call." A confused Norman, "How!? But I called to Dryden, Lord Taurean, who has sent you? The great Dryden?" Taurean replies, "No young Norman, he has not, I received your call, your mighty tone, Tore-Ri-N!" Norman chuckles a bit, "Haha! No master Bull, we called to the great one, Dry-den, maybe the pronunciation caused somewhat of a confusion. Taurean huffs in a chuckle, "Ah, haha, yes,

I see the confusion was my error. Well now that I'm here, I beg you to rid your concern of Dryden." Taurean explains, "Many Gods and beings interact with mortals in many different ways. An example young Norman, the mother you were deeply concerned with, is no mere mortal. She is Lordstress Etoile, a Goddess among glamour and expression. She is a kin of mine. She's here to watch over her son which is the son of George, one of the sons of Cephalos."

Norman looks to the skies, with a disappointed smirk, Taurean could tell this brought on more questions. Taurean speaks, "I implore you, do not waste your time with him, he can barely hear you. He's busy with galaxies or translations or duties. How many more fields of wheat and cotton and berries you need to pick before realizing they will never change. This tactic you're attempting will get you killed much sooner for sure. What you need is to make a statement Norman. A Godly statement! This will for sure bring you triumph!" Norman looks on in response, "What does a Godly statement look like?" Taurean replies, "You have to hit them in their heart, take something of value or concern!" Norman wasn't too sure about this strategy, but felt there was no other option since Dryden was a no show.

"There is a moment in time an opportunity where you can overcome this obstacle. There is a time and day to strike. When the soil is moist in the morning. Perfect enough to rip Flora from the soft soil. That next morning, Norman woke earlier than normal. He laid there on his quilt thinking to himself, "Maybe this isn't so bad, maybe I bit off more than I could chew." Fighting his urge to lay still, Norman jumps up and makes his way towards the hill that laid Flora. Norman left without shoes, seeing as how his wet feet would avoid making noise on moist soil. Arriving, Norman pauses for a minute to admire Flora. Suddenly, out of the darkness, Taurean appears, "Yes! You have held yourself to your word, something Godly!" With one hand, Norman pulls against the Flora. Veins pulsating, he begins

to use both hands to try and pull the plant. Taurean, looking on, yells in a whisper, "Stronger!" Taurean watching in disappointment, "Let me at it," pushing Norman to the side to pluck Flora himself. As Norman falls back onto the wet soil, Cephalos appears, a fur headed beast with several hands and sets of eyes, draws out a blade called the Jeramis. A sharp triangle tip sword used to fight against Gods. The sword drops over Taurean's arm, slicing it off instantly! Taurean's arm, still holding Flora tightly as a sudden burst of wind blows in. Dryden suddenly appears, before a second blow from Cephalos.

Dryden quickly grabs the blade from dropping onto his son's neck while Norman looks up shocked and scared. He struggles, dragging the hand with Flora. Heavy and off balance, Norman makes a run for it down the heel into the woods. Cephalos sends his mortal Lords after Norman as he cradles the arm. Norman makes his way back to the other Nero slaves professing that he has Flora. Bojack as angry as he wanted to be, was impressed. Many of the slaves were happy to see Norman make a stand against Cephalos until the consequences became prevalent. Cephalos warns Norman that the longer he keeps Flora, the more destruction and damage will be done to *his* people.

Dryden met with Norman in the woods with the arm. "What do they call you young master?" Dryden speaks to anxious Norman, "Ah, umm, ahh! They call me Norman, my real name is Normandie." "And so young Normandie, you have taken on great a task, a task fit for a God. The burden of being a harborer of not just life, but death. Are you aware of the true power Florence possesses? Norman stands there in a puzzled look as Dryden explains, "She is a Goddess of growth and all things living, Florence has taken many forms, but the form for mortals is to provide rich soil and bountiful provisions. I know it was my son who has provoked a thought of rebellion. I ask you, what are you to do with Florence while Cephalos lays harsh punishment to your fellowman?" An unsure Norman re-

sponds, "To be honest, I haven't thought much, not since I seen a real God with my own eyes. It was for the first time I felt a sense of importance and concern from my peers. They praised me!" Dryden speaks calmly, "Yes, praise is good and what are you to do with praise, you gave your praise away carelessly to a God whom had no knowledge of your name until moments ago. I reckon to do what you please with Florence, you have earned it. I leave you now and with this, take credit, good or bad. You must remain courageous even in moments of no praise or satisfaction."

Normandie looks up at this huge God, hair wooly and face stern, he speaks in a low tone, "If I may ask Lord Dryden, I ask that one day in passing, my God can acknowledge me." A few days later, the slaves gather around the hill to see that the plant was restored back to its original roots. Weeks past, and one by one the slaves that remained started to drop like flies. Their stomachs were infected with dye and their flesh started to eat away at them. The roots that gave life, now brought death to the land. This forced Cephalos son, to free his remaining slaves due to the foundation of land becoming infected. The remaining slaves followed a path of the mortal who shown a trail to the North. On their way up, many of the slaves lost desire and grew exhausted. These slaves arrived at George's brother plantation, Benjamin. Benjamin's plantation was the closest thing to freedom. Benjamin, to some slaves, was seen as more welcoming as work conditions weren't as strenuous as their previous stay on George plantation The Nero slaves haven't seen Norman since the day before he planted Flora back in the soil. After killing some of their kin, the slaves felt Norman was to blame for their suffering and no one seen Norman again.

Noir, a God who shown unlimited capabilities. He was considered perfect to his tribesman. Noir was one of the last remaining warrior Gods. He was in charge of the safe keeping of Paieun. Noir often traveled to the Sun, covering himself with alluvial and volcanic lava exclusively from Congo. These elements protected Noir soul and body upon landing on the Earth's Sun. What he would often retrieve is Boron, element known to bring forth growth and maintenance in bones. He was noted for being the God that inspired Icarus to sore towards the Sun.

However, Noir never needed wings, he earned the ability to elevate himself upon command over centuries of self-confidence. At this time, God, Arbetai of the Efé and Mtubj people and deity Chorum and Akongo were the Supreme Gods. Noir mostly answered to Akongo, who was supreme of them all, maker of man and earth. Akongo had a daughter Mbokomu, she was the ancestor of all people. Akongo kept Noir by his side to delegate task, command his army and organize battle strategies. Noir was praised among all. Akongo knew he could send Noir to Mbokomu to watch over her as she gives birth to two deities. The first was a boy, Akongo was truly proud. The second was a girl, a deity strong and precious. This one, Akongo grew curious towards. The young one contained a great deal of energy and Boron that Akongo has never seen before. Akongo ordered. Noir, "My young master I need you to watch over this one," pointing to young Paieun.

Noir spent centuries with Paieun, reading her, training her, guiding her. She grew to be a great Goddess. Mbokomu often troubled her father in the immortal lands. Whether it be to watch her young ones or fuss over her birthright to one day be the Supreme. Nevertheless, Mbokomu and her young is released into the mortal worlds as punishment. As an accidental side effect, Noir is cast into the mortal world to chaperon the young Paieun. They brought their clothing, food and architecture to the motherland.

During their stay within the land, Mbokomu noticed slight vulgar Latin dialect of men now occupying the land. Mbokomu began to feel a Godly curiosity, wanting to follow them to a land in which they arrived from. Noir guides the mother and her young to the land of the French, who favored Apollo and Mars for centuries. Noir was aware of the threat of being in a land of creative and war deities. Weary of being a threat, Noir changes his appearance amongst the Frenchman. Noir exposed himself, appearing to speak French, but with a Kongoian dialect. When Noir realized his adaptation was alarming, he instantly returned to his true self. Many of the Gods that roamed the French lands were upset with Noir presence but dared to fight the head Nero in charge and number two to the Supreme, Akongo.

The natives observed and gossiped often, as Noir began to populate the land of France with interracial young. A day soaking the Sun's energy in a valley, a farmer ask Noir, "Why can't you return to your home, your ruining our soil of woman". Noir laid there, looked down on the man, replying, "Ditto!" Young Lords began to form and became ancestor to many Nero people of France and Basque and parts of Italy today. Noir also possessed the ability of foresight, predicting an opportunity or obstacle several steps ahead. His foresight was that of a mortals lifespan, equal to one hundred and two years. Noir, still with this gift, could not see the inevitability of becoming an example for the laws of the lands in later America, known as, "Code Noir".

This code was implemented mainly due to a rumor of a Nero child brought into the womb of Volupta. A Goddess and daughter of Cupid. Louis Dieudonne or as many may know, Louis XIV. Louis shared a great deal of love for Volupta's father and knew he would be devastated if he found out of his daughter interracial affairs. What was true was Cupid did not discriminate of race or color, for his only objection, was imbalance of love. Louis acted in ordering, "Code Noir" within the French American lands and

islands along with Louisiana. Louis wanted Noir killed but such a request was beyond possible, even for a King. Instead, Louis decides to go with his savage instinct and kidnaps Paieun, the daughter of the Goddess Mbokomu.

Paieun would have been equivalent to a 16-year old professional female swimmer at the time. Louis decides to have his way with her and demand Noir leaves France and their woman alone. Louis wife, the Queen of France, wasn't too pleased with the double standards and often laid with Noir when the two were idol. Noir, laying with Louis' wife, would bring cane to his chambers, a temptation that would end the life and times of Louis XIV. Prior to this mortal death, Louis orders Paieun to be shipped along with her Nero slaves to the island, Jamaica. Noir vowed to find Paieun, going along in the path to were the ships are sailed. Paieun often wore no clothes, a symbol of purity. She did, in moments, dress in a beaned necklace and shells amongst her chest and around her torso. On the small boat, Paieun is greeted and praised by Mtumbj and Akan people. Most of them spoke in secret of their native Kongo languages. Some learned French and Patwa.

Policing the Nero along the journey was Iladyse, a God and son of Cephalos. Iladyse grew a strong infatuation with Nero culture. The instruments, such as drums exclusively created by the people of Congo centuries ago. Paintings, clay vases, jewelry, furniture, and weapons of the Congo Nero fascinated Iladyse. Once Paieun arrived to the lands, she bows to one knee drawing a circle in front of her to bless her entry. She noticed many Nero slaves also worshiped a young boy that appeared to be no older than a mortal age of 13. They called him young Legba. His true name learned later was Lufkin. He was alluring. He was given the name for his foresight and guidance. He often would gather Neros at sea that became caught by the tides. His ability to calculate a stroke or misstep was highly rewarded. The natives praised him by roasting crabs, building boats, and offerings of starfish juice.

Lufkin favored those who arrived to the land with children. He saw this as a courageous step forward to think selfless and want more for the children instead of the adults themselves. Many men on the land took advantage of this blessing and began to have several children, hoping for Lufkin to help lead the way. In many cases, Lufkin became disgusted with mortals who saw childbirth as an opportunity to gain immortal favors. When blessing was not given, the slaves often prayed to Paieun during her stay on the island with cowrie shells, which were a form of currency. They also believed the shells brought great fortune, seeing as Paieun was starting to show she is soon to birth a newborn.

Lufkin would sometimes approach Paieun during the golden hours of the day. Providing insight to the land and where he can be helpful towards Paieun. "I see you're due any day now," Lufkin speaks while bringing Paieun a porcelain cup filled with coffee. Lufkin speaks, "The Nero pulled these beans for Louis and his Queen. I wonder what is your plan to leave the land." Paieun speaks as she sips the fresh coffee. "It's not a matter of a plan, I know my mother and guardians have something in store for me. Currently, I am here to watch over my people and assist with any spiritual need." Lufkin request, "Understandable, but if I may allow you to see a path more probable." Paieun accepts without words as he draws a circle around her aura and hums a chant. "If I may, I need a pinch of your blood," Lufkin again requests. She pricks her finger with a shell from her necklace. Lufkin, takes her blood along with a personal item of hers and water from the land and pours them all into the path drawn around Paieun. Lufkin kneels, facing the direction of home, he prays and speaks once again in his native tongue. He then erupted in excitement, "I see, I see a possible! A path you may go towards. A man will come to you, he will bring forth a love that he has never shown to a woman before. He will show you the ways of a male alpha. One thing I see, is that at first what may appear to be chaos, is this man restoring order!"

Paieun, interrupts with a sarcastic chuckle, "Ah-ha! A man! My mothers relationships are examples of men causing trouble and bringing no sort of order. My grandfather kicked us out of our home because of my mother and her *strong mindedness*. Haha! A man! The last thing I need in my life! A true master you are Lufkin!" The following days, Iladyse comes to Paieun to inform her people that some of them will be headed to *Amerigo*, a place many Gods of Latino or Spanish origins believed to be what is known, as America.

The West African Nero were shackled and rushed onto a smaller boat. Lufkin helps Paieun aboard the boat as he takes a pause to look up. He then speaks, "Goddess Paieun! Do you hear a call!?" Lufkin often would hear calls to many Gods. Many of the Nero slaves wanted to surround Paieun, as she began to give birth during their departure. Lufkin lays a cloth made from banana skin weaved together for the arrival of her child. A ceremony of this tradition was not allowed through the guise of Louis XIV generals, although, Iladyse wasn't opposed to it. The slaves brought forth food as an offering, including, fish, tails from cattle and oysters.

Paieun is sung to by the Nero, giving her a peaceful meditative journey through her birth. Lufkin calls out, "The head, the head of our new Queen!" As Paieun pushes, a daughter arrives on board. In the joyous moments, Lufkin, as he is removing the placenta, hears a voice again. On his arm lays a spider trying to gain his attention. "Agh, uh, I can't hear you!" Lufkin replies frantic. It was Anansi, the God of Mischief. He elevates louder, "Noir is coming!" As quickly as he could shout, the ship suddenly explodes. Instantly, all of the slaves and captains are thrown into the sea. Lufkin is thrown in the air with Paieun's baby. Before falling he wraps the newborn in the banana woven, as she lands above the sea line. Iladyse, is also thrown at sea, neglecting the Nero, fleeing with Nero personal affects. The explosion pushes the remaining parts of the boat towards the direc-

tion of Southlands in America. Some of the Nero men begin to swim towards the depths of the oceans as Lufkin looks on in confusion. He hears a cry, a cry growing louder. He flips burnt wood over from the cargo to see a half-women, half-octopus clinging to the underbelly of boat debris. She went along by many names, but referred to herself as Isabel. She confessed her love for the caffeine that was produced through coffee beans. She left her home in Colonna to follow the many facets of coco beans plucked by the Nero. "I want to see the land in which Amerigo speaks of, I hear there are fields of coco beans to feast on. Can you guide me in the right direction," Isabel requesting of Lufkin. "Sorry I can't help you now, I am lost at sea as well, you shall do just find, men of sorts shall help you find your desires," as Lufkin turns the board back on it's side.

Paieun could hear her child cries for her, as she floats closer to Lufkin. A sarcastic Paieun ask, "Is this something you've envisioned?" The hovering Lufkin replies "I operate on diverse streams of time and so I can not always see what's right in front of me." Laughing while wiping water off her face, Paieun replies, "Simply put, you're a child with a wide imagination and you can't seem-" Suddenly, a dark figure comes down! Paieun turns, as she calls out a name in amazement, "Noir!!" It is you! You have returned!" Noir grabbing Paieun with one arm as his body steams the water after the sea touches his feet. Paieun looks at Lufkin, and with a certainty of a smile and knowing, she knew Noir was the man Lufkin mentioned. She looks at Lufkin, "Please watch over my daughter. Take her to a new land. I will return to her. My grandfather will not approve of a love for a child who is part Nero and part Latin." As Paieun reaches her arm out to console her newborn, Noir pulls her and speaks. "I did not intend to blow the whole ship, I simply was trying to disable the rudders." Paieun being carried away replies, "No need for the apology Noir, I am not harmed and to the Nero that were lost, they gave in to the call of a siren. The cries, the flame from wood and soul of the Neros began to fade from the surface of the sea. All that remained was Paieun's daughter and Lufkin. "She didn't even give you a name, what luck do I have?" Lufkin talking aloud just enough to believe the newborn could comprehend. Lufkin surface level confidence begins to feel a mortal grasp of gravity pulling him. The fatigue of his muscles began to weigh him down. He shouts "Ehh-" falling under the sea. Lufkin falling, lands onto an otter chewing on flesh and bone. The otter turns in anger, holding onto Lufkin before he plummets into dark sea. "And who might you be, young child!?" The otter ask with a bushy brow-ridge and sharp triangular teeth. Fatigued Lufkin demanding. "No! Who are you!?" Lufkin concludes, "The thought of an otter who knows language of the Nero!"

"I'm Daigu', a tired exhausted ol'otter. I navigate these seas. I have taken the best of gator, crawfish and monster-oh wait, what's this!? I see you have some tending to above water." Daigu tosses Lufkin towards the surface to check on the newborn. Lufkin was able to notice Paieun's new born develop a force field around herself to avoid danger. As he floats back into the sea, Daigu grabs him once again. "Your arms need rest at the moment, I reckon. You know this isn't a good place to get tired. The sharks here have a path through these channels since the beginning of Nero trade. These waters have build mountains of your people beneath us." "Allow me," Daigu grabs the irate God-child from falling. Daigu brings the young God, Lufkin to the surface. Inhale, Daigu repeats, "Inhale! Exhale! Rest your eyes." Daigu lays Lufkin on the fresh sheet of sea and pulls him left and right. Lufkin laying, begins to float. "If your gonna survive, you'll need to learn how to swim again. I can feel your energy drained." Daigu technique helped the Lord learn how to preserve miles of sea travel. "Now, rest your arms and allow the waves to caress your back," Daigu replies as he cradles over the young Goddess makeshift carriage. They spent a

full day in the Sun training. Daigu confesses, "I'll let you in on a secret. I want to head to the new lands! I hear it's an abundance of opportunities."

Lufkin gathers an idea of the new land through Daigu stories. Sail boats and *feathered men* migrating through the land. "Unfortunately, for me, I haven't had the opportunity to meet the gatekeepers of the south to grant me a great deal of passage," Daigu continues. "How about this!? I take the young Goddess to the land and come back for you. Right now you won't be able to make it to the lands with us, due to your fatigue." Lufkin contemplates the scenario. His foresight began to fade as he had to simultaneously focus on his aquatic relearning. Lufkin didn't have much to think about, seeing as how the young Goddess, akin to Mbokomu, was well needed of rest and food. So he figured just that, telling Daigu, "Yes, alright yes, you may take the young one, her name is Eve, I named her after her circumstance. A name that introduces a beautiful darkness." Daigu allows Lufkin to say a farewell, leaving the young with a shell bracelet and a gold fish necklace, as he promise to return to Lufkin in the soonest hour to come.

Lufkin waits hours upon Godly hours. He begins to seep into the sea once more. He shouts, "Arghh-" falling in. He begins to fall slowly, yet, at a steady pace, to the bottom. Lufkin attempted for several days and weeks of saving energy to rise to the top of the surface once again. One day Lufkin tried to make an attempt and slipped, tumbling until he reached a space at the bottom of the sea displaced from complete light. Lufkin begins to let off a dark blue glow, allowing to see his way, visibly. A mighty rumble reaches Lufkin, as he pivots to prepare for whatever force may arrive. Pallas, a Goddess and messenger of the sea and great granddaughter of Poseidon. A teal chiffon fabric draped the Goddess, as she approaches with a shield. "And who shall I be welcoming to my spear and shield," Pallas replies. Lufkin steps back, "No one! I am here, not as threat but as an unlucky."

Lufkin tries to gauge the Goddess intentions, "Are you a friend of the otter as well, you don't seem as social!?" Pallas thinks briefly, "You mention Daigu, he is cursed to this sea, his true name is Potis, a God of Supremacy and kin to Drogheda. He has been trapped out here until he can provide a offering to the Gods of Land. I bargain he has tricked you into giving your offer to him. This explains why you are now here. Haha, ah goodness, don't feel bad, you're still a boy at heart!" Pallas puzzled, "How can one, being of dark man-boy, sit beneath the sea without crumbling of their body? The young God replies, "The pressures of the sea, land and air are no worry for me. I believe the problem is staying afloat, whether land or sea, but if I may address, I am no mere man-boy, I am Lufkin! God of Sight, God of Perseverance, God of Message."

The Goddess grins and laughs, "Ha, ah, yes, I am something of a messenger myself," Pallas continues. "I am here because I heard a call from the North of a name Lufkin, I now know you are him. You should not stay down here much longer, my sea monsters can eat even a God and a God your size may not last a long meal. Even the sharks still follow the trails of the fallen slaves who fought and died here. You should go! My Grandfather swims to these areas around the time of the warmer seasons. Now, I will do this, I will provide an ally of mine to keep you afloat for some time." Pallas did as said, she sends Lufkin back up with her starfish. Lufkin was able to send a message from one of Pallas creatures in hopes of finding the God otter. Within moments, the otter arrives fixing to build an excuse. "Ah Lufkin, you are in best of shape. I see you made friends with Pallas! I came back, but when I arrived later that day I did not smell you in sight!"

Lufkin replies, "Why did you lie Daigu!?" Daigu rushes to explain himself and then switches into a state of anger, "Look young God-boy, I owe you no reasoning nor rebuttal!" Daigu explains in a rage, "You are a God, but still in

the phase of that of a boy!" As Daigu brushes away, Lufkin shouts, "WAIT! I need to return! There are matters of the child that needs tending! Where is she! Is she safe!?" Daigu shouts back, "She's great Lufkin she's a Goddess in her own right!" Lufkin replies quickly, "Your word is no longer trusting. Uneasy Daigu replies, "I can understand your frustration and I am deeply sorry, but I had to take the opportunity to get off this sea! If I can make a suggestion once more. There is a God, akin of mind, that can protect you. He possesses the ability to make you invisible to most Gods who are the gatekeepers of the new land. He can cast a spell, one powerful enough where your actions or doings won't trouble their environment. However, a favor will be needed from you to provide this spell. I hear you possess the gift of foresight to the mind of a mortal and even Lords and Gods." A cunning Daigu grins. "That's the agreement, your foresight for this spell!"

As foolish as it sounds, Lufkin was in a tough space, yet again. Lufkin kneels his head down in disappointment, "Damnit! Alright! He preforms a ritual to gain Daigu a path. He calls on his ancestors. Though he couldn't conjure anything from the fatigue in his body, he remembered what Pallas mentioned of the otter and his legacy. "A woman in your life will be ruler, a young warrior with the blood of a Titan…" Daigu pushes back, shocked! "I knew it," he replies aloud to himself. And so it was, Lufkin was brought to the land to move amongst the land in stealth. The enchantment on Lufkin it only lasted a few hours a day, so Lufkin regularly stayed near the ocean. Arriving in Southlands, Lufkin developed exclusive relationships with some Neros. Especially during ceremonial events, Lufkin possessed the ability for love ones to send a message to nonliving mortals. He was also able to provide a gift of sight within some of his believers while they were at rest. For some of the mortals who were favored by Lufkin, were able to travel through their dream states into different realms. A skill that took some decades to master. After a few days, Lufkin gained knowledge of

Paieun's daughter location. Lufkin was brought into a small town, a town name, Claude Tremé. It was the start of the oldest Nero town to present time. New Orleans had slaves but became the oldest city for Nero Americans. Paieun's daughter was the first Nero woman to arrive to the lands. Her initial arrival was to a small city, now called Jamestown. She coexisted with farmers and slaves and free Nero alike. She spoke the language of the Nero-Latin and Creole people there. The Nero natives came into wealth there in town from agriculture. It was also there, she met a lover, a man named, Carzara and brought forth children and offspring. She moved with him down to Tremé to build the city for the Nero and Nero Gods.

Inspired by the folklore of Paieun and her daughter, pioneers such as Marcus Garvey, created symbols that were passed down from his grandfather who was a slave on the island of Jamaica when Paieun arrived, witnessing her marvel. The early generation of Nero slaves spoke a very traditional language. These groups were not able to pray to the Nero Goddess, because her language was not of there's. Most older Nero sung songs to their Gods. The younger Nero who wanted to communicate with their ancestors, needed their words to be heard. When they prayed they prayed in English. For most Gods, the language you spoke aloud, is the language they hear in prayer from your heart. This demand and prayer, led to the birth of the God of Language, Dryden, who became a translator for the Nero. Paieun's daughter was the Supreme Goddess of the Nero American. She brought blessings to the free Nero and Nero slave alike. She was the Goddess of Bloodline, connecting every Nero, in the new land, after her, to roots of the Supreme, Akongo. She brought to the land, structure and diet in the form of spirituality. The natives began to knit symbols of her. A dark shade of yellow fabric, woven and stitched of her face, along with four elements that make up the connection of this Amerigo Goddess. Turmeric, sunflowers, wheat, corn, and honey, and even beehives them-

selves were a few examples of offerings in praise to this Goddess. Some Nero mortals were gifted hair from the Nero Goddess as blessings. Many of the future Nero, often confused Eve's favor with an Asian Goddess, due to their similarities in pigment and hair texture. Paieun's daughter was a long-haired Goddess and wore a cuirass made of brass, shells and metal, with an embossed head on the chest, of whom, may be a version of her mother or her grandmother Mbokomu. She never carried a weapon, but casually had a branch or tweak that held berries or fruit. Prior to ceremonies, the natives called her of Eve, a name given in light of appearing in front of them. She often spoke candidly, "Behold, I am here to help the misguided, the confused, the sure, and unsure. The loved and unloved, I am here to bring life to the Nero and remind you of your strength from Akongo himself." Eve is told by one of the Nero about a man who is beloved by Nero fisherman. Lufkin arrives with gifts. A pearl, starfish leg, an a oxtail. Lufkin walks with Eve through her courtyard for Nero to congregate which is now known, as Congo Square.

As they continue, they arrive to a ceremonious graveyard. Eve stops Lufkin from entering with her hand in front of him, "Many realms require a blessing. In this land, no mortal, nor God or other spirit, shall enter a space without proper blessings and offerings. Most think they do not need to provide an offering. A blessing or offering of the gatekeepers who are of Chitimacha Tribe is needed when entering these lands. If not practice, this leaves one's life unstable and somewhat impossible to live, let alone survive." Eve continues to say, "When coming into a dead space always bring something living. Hand me your necklace. A fish! A true gift for the deceased, it shall bring their living families a gift of abundant newborns! I have heard you waited years to return to me. Though, I was only a child, I saw in your heart, your true agenda. The otter didn't just make a trade for me, but a trade for you. He was a prisoner to the sea. It was said that he went against the French and Dutch Gods to pursue his selfish

agendas in the new land. He was turned to a otter as a curse. Once he arrived to the land, his true form displayed a tall an lanky, pale faced deity.

His hands massive, as his arms are elongated and his head was seen as bigger than his body. The otter you've met, is Potis. He arrived with the blessing of southern land natives and gain access to certain parts of the land. He began to build a city for his believers in a town, called *Trimountaine*. Knowing I was a Goddess, this gave him access to speak with tribal Gods and make treaties, as his offering to the land was a Nero women. He only taught you how to swim, so you can be a better swimmer amongst your new home. He was preparing you to be his replacement. There is a world here for the Nero, where we do not rely on any one else but our own. We grow our own crops, blessings of the Goddess, Orizah. We speak our own language, blessing of Lord Dryden. It is *I*, your Goddess, who brings a fertility upon a new race of Nero and now you, my young God-King, Lufkin, to show us the way. Centuries to come, we will be the Gods of the new world, to show our mortal successors a history of strength, righteousness, and independence. They will know we are a fierce and a bold spirit and race. Show them the way Lufkin, you also possess the ability to guide the misshapen, the misguided, and uninformed to a path of comprehension and future."

A tearful Lufkin looks up to Eve, she wipes his tears and replies, "As a God, you have also faced spiritual turbulence in the midst of deciding right from wrong or life or death. You have surely made a Godly sacrifice. To remove me from the sea and hope for my protection was all I can ask." Eve concludes, For this, I shall bless you in my favor, for all of my existence!" Lufkin informs Eve of his curse of invisibility that will soon fade. They walked back to the ocean to stand in the sea. Embracing each other with a hug, Lufkin drifts away with a praise, calling to Eve, "To my God- Our Lady Eve! Long Live the Queen!"

Moving into the new centuries, these aging Gods begin to compete with deities of a Cyborg Era. After the death of Lesane, many of the Nero Gods from the Revolutionary Era managed to survive with Henos becoming heir and leader for the Nero mortals. The Goddess, Aria was later worshiped out west. Primarily used for a resort, a building was erected in her name. As for her sister, Etoile, her name was praised through an accessory line. Darious, Piruphius' close engineer and craftsman eventually teaches a young Demi-God, Ye the ways of his mastery. He favored him because of Ye's father who was a photographer for Dryden and Piruphius' Tribesmens and key for archiving Darious' work. Deities born from the God Henos, govern the realms of Hip-Hop culture for the Nero. Much of Henos offspring paved the way for the future generation. Eventually, Henos was met with his rumored death, this caused the birth of his offspring called, the Goons. They were aimless deities whom expressed anger for the lack of attention from their father, Henos.

For Elbrus Gods, Goddess like Madonna, spawn a new Lordestress, such as Gaga, a Goddess of Musical Pop. Chera, Goddess of Pop, offers a powerful favor to arriving Nymphs, known as the Shians. Drogheda is crowned Supreme Goddess over all Orcheus, after a March for their sexual and independent freedoms. Medusa was awaken by the Nero who embraced her, due to Lesane's relationship with her. After her return, she initially felt distant from Nero believers. It isn't until later, she sees Nero's stealing garments and jewelry of her during future protest and riots. Understanding the sacrifice their willing to make for her.

Juniper and Nike become Supreme Gods in the new America. Nike apparel brand sores into a cultural lifestyle. Ignacia, Nike's alter ego becomes noticeable around worlds even outside of Nero communities. For her protégé Michael, grows to become a distant God, not partaking too

much in mortal affairs. The strategy for Gods like Potis in this new era is to realign his followers to follow him into a "Great America again." In order to accomplish this, he forms a idea to reinforce a segregation against Nero having a voice politically, financially and now more than ever socially.

His brother Oculus, has a child with Josephine's daughter, Onelia. It is this birth that breeds Thais, the God of New Media and Social Gathering. Thais becomes the youngest, most influential and impressionable deity during the inception of the Cyborg Era. He alone begins to feed off the conditioning and addiction of mortals. Thais has several offspring including, Goddess of Fame Gloriosa, a God in a deep romance with Gaga. Another sibling is God of Change and Constant, Cipha. Thais and their siblings breed a half God, half Cyborg by the name of Troon. With these elements growing into dominance, Gods like Orizah, Etoile, and Taurean are essential cultural attache' who practice cultural morale and principal while many of the Nero Gods fade out or integrate with Elbrus Gods, clinging to existence. This marriage between two groups of deities breeds a God of half-man and half-bird that brings about the future God, Ovol.

ACKNOWLEDGMENT

THE WALKS IN ITHACA on Dryden road to the river trail. Managing others insecurities ...Those important PHONE CALLS... the organizations that charge a fee to access transatlantic slave data...southern plantations creating profitable tours to visit our historic land.. understanding how much more of healing I need. the distractions..THE ENERGY..reading energy from others as well as myself.. THE SUPPORT FROM MY MOTHER... the time walking in RH... THE TIME I don't have vs time I do.... THE DISAPPOINTMENT FROM BLACK PEERS who want change but are afraid of it...my anger for lack of identity...the nights i wanted to give up but the days i wanted to pursue.. BETTY!-writing most of the work in the backseat ....my grandmothers journey and her mother running from the south....my grandfathers life and journey...my focus, true focus on one small idea and resisting the urge to burst into several different projects beyond my capacity ....my dedication my drive my perseverance....the bondships of those who decided to show interest and support in this lifelong project...my journey.... Kev Mac, Black Tribe Researcher & Historian for provided insight of a culture deeply misunderstood yet globally embraced.

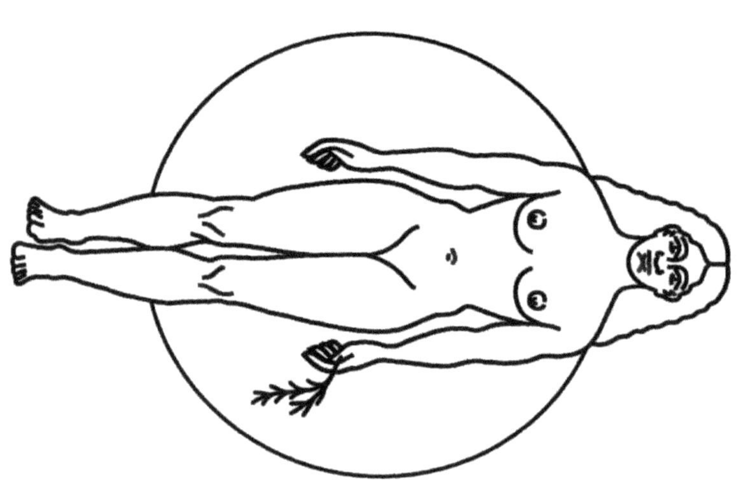